McPHEE GRIBBLE/PENGU

HOME TIME

Beverley Farmer was born in Melbourne in 1941 and educated at MacRobertson Girls' High School and Melbourne University. She has supported herself since through a variety of jobs. For three years in Greece she lived a village life, taught English and helped run a seaside restaurant. She recently completed a term as writer-in-residence at the University of Tasmania. She likes reading, music, cycling and films. She lives partly in Melbourne and partly in Point Lonsdale and has a thirteen-year-old son. Her first novel, *Alone*, was published in 1980. Beverley Farmer's award-winning story collection, *Milk*, was published in 1983. At present she is writing full-time.

by the same author
MILK
ALONE

HOME TIME

stories by
BEVERLEY FARMER

Published with the assistance of the
Literature Board of the Australia Council

McPHEE GRIBBLE/PENGUIN BOOKS

McPhee Gribble Publishers Pty Ltd
66 Cecil Street
Fitzroy, Victoria, 3065, Australia

Penguin Books Australia Ltd,
487 Maroondah Highway, P.O. Box 257
Ringwood, Victoria, 3134, Australia
Penguin Books Ltd,
Harmondsworth, Middlesex, England
Penguin Books,
40 West 23rd Street, New York, N.Y. 10010, U.S.A.
Penguin Books Canada Ltd,
2801 John Street, Markham, Ontario, Canada L3R 14B
Penguin Books (N.Z.) Ltd,
182-190 Wairau Road, Auckland 10, New Zealand

First published by McPhee Gribble Publishers
in association with Penguin Books Australia, 1985
Copyright © Beverley Farmer, 1985

Typeset in Bembo by Bookset, Melbourne
Made and printed in Australia by
The Dominion Press–Hedges & Bell

National Library of Australia
Cataloguing-in-Publication data

Farmer, Beverley, 1941-
Home time.

ISBN 0 14 008677 3.

I. Title.

A823'.3

For Taki

Φτενὸ στὰ πόδια σου τὸ χῶμα
    γιὰ νὰ μὴν ἔχεις ποῦ ν᾽ ἁπλώσεις ρίζα
    καὶ νὰ τραβᾶς τοῦ βάθους ὁλοένα

let the soil at your feet be thin
    so that you will have nowhere to spread roots
    and have to delve in the depths continually

Odysseus Elytis, *To Axion Esti* from *Genesis*

ACKNOWLEDGEMENTS

Acknowledgement is made to the publications in which these stories first appeared: 'Caffe Veneto' in *Follow Me*; 'The Harem' in *Australian Short Stories*; 'A Woman with Black Hair' in *Social Alternatives*; 'Market Day' in *Australian Short Stories*; 'White Friday' in *Outrider*; 'A Man in the Laundrette' in The *Australian Literary Supplement*; 'Marina' in *Tabloid Story*; 'Pomegranates' in The *Canberra Times*; 'Our Lady of the Beehives' in *Meanjin*.

CONTENTS

PLACE OF BIRTH

ON THE last day Bell will remember before the snow, on a blue-grey morning of high cloud, the old woman brings out a *tapsi* rolling with walnuts that she has cracked for the Christmas *baklava*. 'We'll be shut in soon enough,' she sighs, perching on a plaited stool under the grapevine with the *tapsi* on her lap. Bell, her son Grigori's wife, pulls up stools for herself and Chloe, the other daughter-in-law, the Greek one who has come to the village for Christmas; her husband's ship is at sea. The women huddle over the *tapsi* picking out and dropping curled walnuts here, shells there. Chloe's little girl, Sophoula, leans on her mother.

'Me too?' she murmurs.

'Go ahead.'

Sophoula, biting her lips, scowls over her slow fingers. With a trill of laughter Chloe pops a walnut into the child's mouth. 'My darling! Eat,' she says.

'Don't tell me she has nuts at her age?' the old woman says. 'You'll choke the child.'

'Mama, she's three.' Chloe's face and neck turn red.

'Just the same –'

'Oh, I don't like it!' Sophoula spits and dribbles specks of walnut. The shelling goes on; under their bent heads Chloe and the old woman put on a fierce burst of speed. Suddenly all of them flare bright with sunlight and are printed over with black branches and coils of the grapevine as a gap opens in the cloud. Bell leaps to her feet and lumbers inside.

'What's wrong with you?' Chloe frowns.

'Nothing. I'm getting my camera.'

'*Aman*. Always photographs,' her mother-in-law sighs.

'It's too cold to sit out here,' Chloe says.

'Oh, please,' Bell wails from the window. 'All stay where you are!'

But the gap in the cloud has closed over by the time she gets back, so that what she will always have is a photograph all cold blues, whites, greys and browns: brittle twigs and branches against walls and clouds, the washing hung along the wire, a white hen pricking holes in mud that mirrors her, and the three heads, black, brown and bone-white, suspended over the *tapsi* of walnuts.

Because she takes all the photographs, she won't find herself in any of them.

Six weeks ago, as soon as she knew for certain, Bell wrote to her parents that they would be grandparents some time in May. 'You're the first to know,' she added, though by the time the letter got to Australia the whole village probably knew. There's no hope now of an answer until after Christmas. But at noon the postman's motorcycle roars past, a fountain of mud in his wake, and stops at the village office, so she wanders down just in case and is handed an Australian aerogram. It has taken a month to get here and is one she will mark with a cross and keep as long as she lives.

Grandma and Grand Pop, eh, scrawls her father. *And about time too. Tell Greg to take that grin off his face.*

'Are they pleased, Bella?' The old woman is kneading the pastry for the *baklava*. Her arms are floured to the shoulders.

'Of course. Dad says, "And about time too."'

'No wonder! Considering that you're thirty-one –'

'Thirty –'

' – or will be when it's born.'

'Hasten slowly.' Bell reads her mother's exclamatory,

incoherent half-page, laboriously copied, then goes back to her father's.

It's been three years. You could leave it too late, you know, Bell. With a bub and all that you could find yourselves tied down before you know it. It's hard to think we mightn't live to see our only grandchild. Mum's been having dizzy turns again lately. She's had one stroke, as you know. If money's the problem, I can help you there. Also book you into the Queen Vic or wherever you like.

'What else, Bella?'

'Oh, questions. Money, hospitals. All that.'

'Surely you're booked into the Kliniki?' Chloe stares.

'No, not yet.'

'Well, you'd better do it soon! You don't want to have it in the Public Hospital! *They* have women in labour two to a bed in the corridors, it's so crowded.'

'I think I want to have it at home,' Bell hears herself say.

'At home!' Kyria Sophia is delighted. 'Why not? I had all mine here. Grigori was born in the room you sleep in!'

'It wouldn't be safe.' Chloe raises her eyebrows. 'Not with a first child. Anything can go wrong.'

'Thank you, Chloe.'

'It's the truth. Look what happened to the *papas*'s daughter!'

'The *papas*'s daughter? You know why that happened? She got a craving for fried bananas in the middle of the night and her husband wouldn't go and try to find her any. And sure enough –'

'Mama, the cord got round her baby's neck and strangled it.'

'Mama, not because of the bananas!'

'You're both fools! Of course it was because of the bananas!' The old woman rams a grey branch into the firebox of the *somba*. '*Aman*! How come I'm the only one who ever stokes the fire?' She brushes a wisp of hair out of her eyes and flours her face. White like her hair and arms, it sags into its net of wrinkles.

Lunch, Bell's chore today, isn't ready when the old man comes in from the *kafeneion* and finds her alone in the kitchen. Kyria Sophia has taken Sophoula with her to the bakery to leave the *baklava*, Chloe is at a neighbour's place with the baby. He sits by the *somba*, small and grey and muddy, rolling and smoking one fat cigarette after another. The *makaronia* have to be boiled to a mush, Bell knows, before she can toss them in oil and butter and crumble *feta* cheese over them. Kyria Sophia comes back exhausted hand-in-hand with Sophoula and as if the day's work wasn't enough, now she has her to spoonfeed.

They eat the *makaronia* in silence. At every mouthful a twinge, a jab of pain drills through Bell's jaw. Not a toothache, please, she prays. Not now, not here.

Sophoula pushes the spoon and her grandmother's hand away. 'Yiayia! You have to tell a story!'

'What story?' sighs the old woman.

'A story about princesses.'

'Eat up and then I will.'

'Now!' Sophoula bats the spoon on to the floor. The old woman gets another one and shovels cold lumps into the child's mouth, chanting a story by heart. Whenever she falters, the child clamps her mouth shut. Bell, stacking the dishes, isn't really listening, but when the bowl is almost empty she exclaims aloud in English, 'Snow White! No, Snow White and Rose Red!'

The old woman giggles. 'Zno Quaeet,' she mocks. 'No Zno Quaeet End –'

'Yiayia, *pes*!'

'*Aman*, Sophoula!'

'*Pes*.' She spits into the bowl.

After lunch these days Bell sleeps until it's dark. Now that she is into her fifth month she is sleepy most of the time. From under the white *flokati* she can hear Grigori's voice (so he is back from Thessaloniki with the shopping) and then Kyria Sophia's shrill one. When she wakes properly, ready for another long yellow evening by the *somba*, he is still there in the kitchen finishing a coffee. So is Chloe, red from her sleep, with the baby at her breast. 'Hullo,' Bell says, kissing Grigori's woolly crown. She fumbles with the *briki*.

'Coffee again?' Chloe mutters.

'Just one to wake me up.'

'It's so bad for the baby.'

'One won't hurt.'

'Oh well, you'd know.'

Bell turns her back to light the gas. 'Where are the old people?' She touches Grigori's shoulder.

'Milking.' His father's grey head grins in at the window; he leaves the milk saucepans on the sill. 'You got a letter, Mama said. Are Mum and Dad all right?'

'Yes, they send their love and congratulations.' Bell rubs her jaw. There's a hollow ache in her back teeth. She empties the sizzling *briki* into a little cup and takes a furry sip of her hot coffee. The *baklava* is on the table, baked and brought home already, its pastry glossy with the syrup it's soaking in. Grigori's shopping is all around it: oranges in net bags, chestnuts, a blue can of olive oil, lemons and mandarines and – she can hardly believe it – six yellow-green crescent bananas blue-stamped *Chiquita*. 'Oh, bananas! Oh, darling, thank you!' she cries out. 'We were just talking about bananas!'

'I'm so extravagant,' Chloe simpers, 'but Sophoula simply loves them. So I gave Grigori the money to buy her some.' Her eyes dare Bell to ask for one. A pregnant woman can ask even strangers in the street for food. Bell grins at Chloe, remembering her frying mussels one day in Thessaloniki when a pregnant neighbour squealed from a

5

balcony, 'Ach, Kyria Chloe! Mussels! I can smell them!' and Chloe had to let her have a couple. 'She never smells anything cheap,' Chloe grumbled to Bell.

'Is that so, Kyria Chloe?' Bell contents herself with saying. 'Ah, so much lovely food. We'll never eat it.'

'*You* won't.' The old woman comes in and lifts the milk saucepans inside. '*Aman*, the cold!' She slams the window. '*You* won't eat. You're fading, look at you. White as snow.'

'I *will*. That was when I had morning sickness.'

'We don't want a kitten, you know, we want a big strong baby.'

'Believe you me,' Chloe mutters, 'the bigger it is, the harder it comes out.'

'Ah, *bravo*, Chloe, *bravo*!' The old woman clatters the saucepans, straining the warm milk. 'Don't you crave anything, Bella? You must crave something.'

'Why must she?'

'Well, to tell the truth, I'd love a banana,' says Bell. 'It seems like years! Can I buy one from you, Chloe?'

'I'm sorry. There aren't enough.'

'We share in this house, Chloe! If you want a banana, Bella, you have one! Don't even ask!'

'No, no, it's all right.'

Grigori stands up. 'See you later,' he says. He grabs a mandarine and saunters outside.

'Not to the *kafeneion* already?' his mother pleads. 'You just got here.' She stares bleakly after him. 'And what would you expect?' She rounds on her daughters-in-law. 'Doesn't a man have a right to peace and quiet?'

'Auntie?' Chloe has taught Sophoula this English word. 'Auntie Bella? Do they have Christmas where you come from?'

'Yes, of course.'

'Did you go to church?'

'No.'

'You stayed home at Christmas!'

'We went to the beach,' Bell says.

'At Christmas! You're funny, Auntie!'

'Funny, am I?' Bell crosses her eyes. With a giggle, Sophoula sits in her lap.

'Where's your baby?'

'You're sitting on it. Oh, poor baby.'

'What's its name going to be?'

'I don't know. What's your baby's name going to be?'

'We won't know till he's been christened.'

'Oh, no, I forgot.'

'If it's a girl, they'll call it after Yiayia,' Chloe interposes. 'The same as we did with you.'

'Good idea. I'll call my baby Yiayia.'

'Auntie, you can't!'

'Why can't I? Not if it's a boy, you mean?' Bell winks. 'Then I'll call it Pappou,' and she is rewarded with a peal of laughter so loud that it wakes the old woman.

'Let's eat, Mama,' Chloe says.

'Is it late?' She blinks, squinting in the light. 'The men'll be home any minute.'

'No, they won't.' Bell lifts Sophoula down. 'Can we cut the *baklava* now? I crave *baklava*.'

'Oh. All right.' Smiling in spite of herself, Kyria Sophia cuts her a dripping slice. As Bell bites into it, the ache that has been lying in wait all day drills through her tooth and she shrieks aloud, letting syrup and specks of walnut dribble down her chin. She swills water round her mouth. The women cluck and fluster. Sophoula clings to her mother in tears of fright. The old woman mixes Bell an aspirin and she gulps it. She is helped to bed, where she curls up moaning in the darkness under the *flokati*. The light flashes on once, twice. She lies still until the door quietly closes.

Grigori is undressing with the light on. Bell rubs her watery eyes. The ache is duller now.

'Were you asleep? How's the tooth?'

'Bad.' She probes with her tongue.

He turns off the light and lies on his back with one cold arm against her. 'What's all this about having the baby here at home?'

'No! I'd be terrified.'

'Mama said you said you wanted to.'

'No. She misunderstood. I meant – I just feel – I want to go home and have it.' She holds her breath. 'Home to Australia.'

'How come?'

'Oh. Mum and Dad. You know. Mostly, I suppose. Yes.'

'We can't afford the fares.'

'One way, we can. Dad said they'd help.'

'Ah. One way? I see.'

The moon must have risen. In the hollow glow through the shutters the *flokati* looks like a fall of snow on rough ground. 'I wonder if it'll snow for Christmas?' she says. 'It didn't the other times.'

He snorts. 'You spring a thing like this on me. What I might feel – you couldn't care less, could you! I wanted to stay in Australia three years ago, but no, you uprooted us, you – *felt* – you had to go and live in Greece. And now what? Come along, doggy, I want to go home. To Australia!'

She takes a shaky breath. 'I feel guilty, I suppose. They're old, they're not well. "You could leave it too late," Dad said.'

'You know what a pessimist he is. You used to joke about it.'

'Can we bank on it, though?' She ploughs on. 'It's not as if it would be for ever.'

'It might.'

'We can always come back.'

'Always, can we? Backwards and forwards.' He turns his back to her. 'I'll need to think it over. I'm tired.'

'There's not much time. We've got till the end of February. That's when my smallpox vaccination expires. I can't have another one while I'm pregnant and I can't enter Australia without it.'

Lying along his back, she feels him tightening against her. The nape of his neck is damp and has his hot smell. Once he pelted past her down a sand dune and was out of sight in the white waves when the hot smell from him buffeted her face. That was at Christmas.

We went to the beach at Christmas when I was little, she remembers. On Phillip Island we had dinner at the guesthouse and then Dad and I followed a track called Lovers' Walk – there was a board nailed up, Lovers' Walk – to look for koalas as they awoke in the trees. First we walked down the wooden pier where men and their sons were fishing. Red water winding and hollowing. Crickets fell silent when I walked in the tea-tree. After sunset the waves were grey and clear rolling and unrolling shadows on the sand. The trees, black now, still had their hot smell.

Some time in the early hours the toothache jerks her out of sleep. Grigori breathes on deeply. Tossing, feverish, close to tears, she stumbles to the kitchen for an aspirin and Chloe, passing through to the lavatory annexe, sees and scolds her. 'You shouldn't take any medicines now,' she says.

'One little aspirin!' Bell's smile is a snarl.

'Any medicine at all.'

'I have toothache!'

'Still, for the baby's sake.'

Bell turns and gulps it down. Back in bed the pain is relentless, it drills into her brain. After an hour, two, of whimpering in her sweat she creeps back to the kitchen and in a flash of bilious light swallows down three more

aspirins. No one catches her. In the passage she trips over
Sophoula's potty, which they leave outside their door until
morning. Splashing away over cold urine, she lets it lie
where it fell. Grigori is snoring. 'Turn over,' she hisses in
Greek, and he turns.

A rooster calls, the same one as every morning, then
hens, then a crow, so loud that it must be in the yard. How
long since she last heard a gull? It must be only a couple of
weeks. When was the last time she was in Thessaloniki?
Gulls are as common as pigeons in the city. It seems like
years.

What does tea-tree smell like in summer?

Their bedroom is white and takes up one corner of the
house and of the street, 21st of April Street these days, in
honour of the Colonels' coup. The two-roomed school
that Grigori went to is opposite. They are on one of the
busiest crossroads in the village. All through Christmas
Day, Boxing Day and the next day Bell sleeps and wakes
to the uproar of tractors, donkeys, carol-singers, carts,
trucks with loud-speakers bellowing in her windows.
Snow falls. She sits sipping milk at the family table in her
pyjamas, staggers to the lavatory annexe and back to her
cooling hollow under the *flokati*. She coughs. Her head
pulsates. She loses count of how many aspirins. The toothache goes through her in waves. Sweat soaks her pyjamas
and sheets and Kyria Sophia dries them again by the *somba*.
Grigori takes refuge for two nights at his cousin Angelo's
place behind the bakery. Children throwing snowballs yell
and swear. The baby wails. From time to time Sophoula
opens Bell's door, but slams it in panic when Bell stirs to
see who it is. Chloe keeps away in case she and the children
catch something. Kyria Sophia comes and sits at the end of
the bed crocheting with a pan of hot coals at her feet.

Penicillin, somebody suggests, a shot of penicillin,
there's a woman down the street who's qualified. Bell says
yes, oh yes, please. Chloe is appalled. But no one ever
comes to give the injection. Time has broken down. Sand

slides shifting under the scorched soles of her feet. The scream of a gull makes her slip and clutch at the stringy trunk of a tea-tree, but it must be the grapevine. No, she is flat on her back, she is clutching the *flokati* when her eyes open. It looks like snow on rough ground. That scream comes again and it's the baby screaming, Chloe's baby though, not her own, that she can hear, then all the sounds of hushing and commotion as he sobs, then whimpering and quiet.

One morning she wakes and is well, clear-headed, free of toothache and of fever. She opens the windows but the shutters won't move. She is weak, look, trembling. But it's not that: snow is heaped on the sill. She patters to the door and stares down the white street. The sun is rising behind white roofs and trees, turning the snow sand-yellow, shading in the printed feet of birds and a stray dog. The stringy grapevine has grown spindles of ice.

Stooped panting over buckets and *tapsia* of water, she spends the day washing her stiff, sour clothes and her hair, stuck in yellow strings to her head by now; and sitting with hair and clothes spread out to dry by the *somba*. She would love a bath, but not in the dank ice-chamber that the lavatory annexe has become. For one thing, other people are always wanting to get in. And in any case, it's not as if they'll notice whether she does or not, not even Grigori: for fear of a miscarriage, now that she has finally conceived they don't make love. She's well again, she won't risk catching cold. She wraps a scarf over her mouth whenever she goes outside. Now and then a twinge through her tooth alarms her, but the rivetting ache is gone.

Every day there is washing and cooking of which she does her share. When the sun is out she walks around the village photographing crystals and shadows, tufty snow and smooth. The narrowed river is crinkled, slow, with white domes on its rocks. Ovens in the deserted yards have a cap of snow over two sooty airvents and stare back at the camera like ancient helmets. White hens are invisible except for their jerking legs and combs. The storks' nest is piled high; it could be a linen basket up on top of the church tower. In the schoolyard a snowman has appeared – no, a snow woman two metres tall in a widow's scarf and a cloak of sacking under which her great round breasts and belly glisten naked.

She takes photographs of the snow woman and of children hiding to throw snowballs and of the *papas* as he flaps by, his hair and beard like a stuffing of straw that has burst out of his black robes. The family and the neighbours line up for portraits under the grey grapevine. The old man leads the cows out of the barn and poses for her standing between them on the soiled snow while they shift and blink in the light, mother and daughter.

'You can show them to your parents,' he says. So all the family knows that she is going home. No one talks about it.

She takes time exposures in the blue of evening as the windows in the houses light up and throw their long shapes on the snow outside. As often as not, Kyria Sophia, Chloe, Grigori, even the old man, can be found in one or other of the rooms, the little golden theatres, that Bell used to love being in. Now she knows the sets, the characters, the parts too well. She would rather stay home alone; she is quite happy babysitting. Having read her own few books too often, she reads Sophoula's story books about princesses. If Sophoula wakes, Bell reads aloud with the warm child in her lap. When the old man comes in they roast chestnuts on top of the *somba* until the others come. They listen in to the clandestine broadcasts on Deutsche Welle, which he calls Dolce Vita: these are banned by the Junta and the penalty for listening could be imprisonment, could be torture. He has enemies who would report him if they knew. 'The walls have ears,' he growls, the radio pressed to his grey head; he is hard of hearing himself. His wrinkles are so deep that they pull his hooded eyes into a slant and his lips into a perpetual smile around his cigarette.

On New Year's Eve Kyria Sophia announces that she is too tired even to dream of making the family *vassilopita*. 'Thank goodness my nephew's the baker,' she says. 'Angelo says he'll bring us one.'

Chloe fluffs up her hair. 'My mother always makes ours.'

'It's a lot of bother for nothing, if you ask me!' snaps the old woman. 'Who appreciates it? Look at all my *baklava* that none of you will eat!'

'Mama, it's a wonderful *baklava*!' Bell hugs her.

'You say that. Eat some then.'

'And what about my tooth?'

'*Aman*, that woman!' Bell hears her whisper to Grigori. 'I could wring her neck,' meaning Chloe, or so Bell hopes.

Then to her further exasperation the old woman looks everywhere and can't find the *flouri*, the lucky coin that she hides in each year's *vassilopita*. Bell gives her the lucky sixpence that she brought from home, the one her mother used to put in the plum pudding.

After dinner, while Grigori and his father are still at the *kafeneion*, Angelo and his mother, Aunt Magdalini, arrive with the *vassilopita*. An elderly doll in long skirts, she falls asleep by the *somba*, steam rising from her woollen socks. Bell wakes her to eat a floury *kourabie*, and again to drink coffee. Angelo has ouzo. It blurs his sharp brown features, so like Grigori's, and makes him jocular.

'What can you see out there, Bella?' She turns from the window. 'Your man coming home?'

'The moon rising.'

'*Fengaraki mou lambro*,' recites Sophoula proudly.

'Good! What comes next?'

'*Fexe mou na perpato!*'

'I'll give you twenty drachmas,' Angelo drawls, 'if you

can tell me what the moon's made of.'

'Rock?'

'You lost. It's a snowball, silly. It was thrown so high it can't ever come back to earth.'

Sophoula's jaw drops. 'Who threw it?'

'Guess.' He scratches the black wool on his head.

'A giant?'

'*I* think a bear. There's one up the mountain. There were tracks up there the other day. The hunters are out after her.'

'The poor bear!'

He peers out the window. 'That's not her in the school-yard, is it? A huge white bear?'

'Silly.' She giggles. 'That's only the snow woman.'

'The snow woman, is it?' hisses Angelo. 'So that's who threw the moon up there!' and Sophoula screams in terror.

Kyria Sophia glares up over her glasses. 'God put the moon there.'

'Supposing she comes alive at night time? Supposing she comes and stares in all the windows while we're asleep?'

'No, no!' Sophoula clamps herself to Bell. 'Auntie, make him stop it!'

'Angelo, please?'

'Of course she doesn't!' cries Kyria Sophia. 'Aren't you ashamed to put an idea like that in the child's head?'

The door bursts open on Chloe red-faced and turbulent. 'You'll wake the baby! Can't I leave you alone here for one minute?' She drags the child by the arm into their room. There they both stay until Angelo and Aunt Magdalini have gone and Grigori and his father are home for the midnight ceremony of cutting the *vassilopita*. Then Chloe sidles sullenly in with her black hair stuck to cheeks still red with sleep or crying. 'Sophoula will have to miss it. She's asleep,' she mutters.

The old man, as head of the household, carefully divides the loaf. He sets aside a piece for the church and then for every member of the family, present and absent. The lucky sixpence turns up in Chloe's baby's piece, as it was bound to, and they all pretend surprise. Bell stuffs the sweet bread into the safe side of her mouth. Next New Year, she knows, wherever they all are by then, the *flouri* or the sixpence will turn up in her child's piece.

The New Year card games at the *kafeneion* will go on all night. Grigori walking back is a shadow among other shadows that the moon makes in the snow.

On New Year's Day no bus comes to the village. The road in has been declared dangerous because the two narrow wooden bridges that it crosses are thick with frozen snow. No buses until further notice, bellows the village loudspeaker. People grumble. This happens every winter and every winter the government promises a new road. The mountain villages are worse off, of course; they'll be snowed in for weeks, not just a few days. Still, since no one has a car, everyone is trapped here while it lasts, except Angelo with his bread van.

Angelo goes on delivering his bread around the villages using chains, risking unmade tracks on hills and across fields to bypass the bridges. Grigori has been joining him lately for the sake of the ride and the company; now he goes on every trip in case Angelo strikes trouble and needs a hand. But Angelo won't take anyone else. 'It's not legal,' he tells everyone, 'and it's not safe.' He broke his rule twice last year, he says, and look what happened. The old man that he took to the district hospital in the back of the van survived; but the woman in labour? She lost her baby when the van hit a buried rock miles from anywhere and broke an axle. 'Never again, not for a million drachmas,' he says. 'Don't ask me.'

So that evening Bell and Chloe, sitting by the small

somba in Chloe's room with the work done and the children asleep, are thunderstruck when Kyria Sophia – who has made herself scarce all day – puts her head round the door to announce that by the way she and Grigori are off first thing in the morning to Thessaloniki to see her other grandchildren. Angelo is giving them a lift.

'She can't do that!' Chloe cries out, and follows her into the kitchen. 'You can't do that!' Bell hears.

'What? What can't I do?'

'What about *me*?'

'What about you?'

'I brought the children all this way to visit you and it wasn't easy on the bus and now you take it into your head to go off to Thessaloniki just like that and –'

'Look, when I need you to tell *me* what –'

' – And leave us stranded here!'

'What would you do there, anyway?' Kyria Sophia shouts. 'Your husband's away at sea for two more weeks!'

'I happen to live there. *Your* husband's here, remember? How will he feel if you go? This is your house, it's not mine. I could have gone to my own village for Christmas and New Year when they begged me to. *My* mother –'

'You're a married woman. It's your duty to come to us.'

'Duty? Oh, duty? What about your duty, then? Aren't *you* a married woman?'

'You dare to talk to me like –'

'Mama, you have *no right* –'

'Get out of my kitchen, Chloe. You say one more word and I swear I'll hit you. I'll hit you!'

Chloe strides into the room where Bell and now Sophoula too are listening in horror; she slams the door behind her. Thuds and crashes of glass hit the wall between them.

'*Oriste mas! Oriste mas!*' come her shrieks. 'Now *she'll* tell *me* if I can go or not, will she? Twenty-five years old! *She'll* tell *me* what I can and can't do?'

'Mama, what's Yiayia saying?' Sophoula whimpers.

'Never you mind. She's wicked. She doesn't love you or any of us.' Chloe bites her lips. 'Let the old bitch howl,' she mutters. 'She would have slapped my face in there! She knows she's in the wrong.'

The outside door slams and they jump. Footsteps splash past the shuttered window. The three of them creep to their beds. Bell is still wide awake when at last Grigori comes in and starts undressing in the dark.

'Grigori?'

'You're awake, are you? What happened here? Mama's in a frenzy. She's beside herself.'

'She had a fight with Chloe.'

'And you?'

'Me? No! I stayed out of it.'

'You didn't try to stop her.'

'As soon try stopping a train! If Chloe wants a fight, I suppose that's her business, isn't it?'

'If she fights with her own mother it's her business. If she fights with mine it's my business and yours and all the family's.'

'So I should have stopped her.'

'You were there.' He has slid into bed without touching her. 'And your place in the family gives you the right.'

'Because I'm older than Chloe?'

'No. Because I'm the older brother and you're my wife.'

'Oh. I think Chloe was right to be upset. Is it fair of Mama to go off and leave us like this?'

'One more day of Chloe, she says, and she'll go mad.'

'Chloe's hard to take. It's the children. They tire her out, you see.'

'Mama does everything.'

'No, she doesn't. Chloe pulls her weight. I'm here all day and I know.'

'*You* know! You live in a world of your own! Chloe pulls her weight, does she? And what about you?'

'Tell me, what do the men do here while the women are pulling their weight? Play cards in the *kafeneion*? Stroll around Thessaloniki? If it comes to that, I'm the one who really needs to go. If I don't get to a dentist, I might lose this tooth.'

'Nice timing.'

'For every child a tooth, they say. It's to do with lack of calcium.'

She feels him shrug. 'Drink more milk.'

'I'm awash with milk already. Milk won't fill a rotten tooth, though, will it?'

'Well, bad luck,' he says wearily. 'It's stopped aching, hasn't it? There'll be a bus soon anyway, go on that. The fact is Angelo only has room for two and he needs me.'

'Well, let *me* come, then! Explain to Mama!'

'*You* explain to Mama.' He waits for her to think that over. 'Why all this fuss, I wonder?'

'You're going and leaving me here.'

'It's not as if it's for ever, is it?'

'Oh, that's it. I see. You want revenge.'

'You're happy to go off to Australia and leave me here.'

'Happy? I'm hoping you'll come.'

'It's more than hoping, I think. It's closer to force.'

They are lying rigidly side by side on their backs and neither moves. 'You'd be taking my child with you.'

She snorts. 'Not much choice at this stage!'

'No. There's not. So I want you to wait.'

'I can't, I told you. My smallpox vaccination.'

'I know that! I mean wait till after it's born.'

She opens her eyes wide in the darkness, so suddenly alarmed that she thinks he will hear the blood thumping through her. 'No. I'd be trapped here then,' she dares to say.

'Trapped!'

'Besides, the whole point is to be home with Mum and Dad before the birth. And then come back. If you want.'

'*Why*? Why does it matter *where* you are for the birth?'

'It just does,' she mutters. 'I'll feel safer there.'

'You're a stubborn, selfish, cold-blooded woman, Bell.

18

You always have been and you always will be.'

'Always?'

'You want your own way in everything. Well, you're not getting it.'

Calming herself, she strokes the long arch of her belly, fingering the navel which has turned inside out and then the new feathery line of dark hair down to her groin. Once or twice a flutter inside her has made her think the baby has quickened, but it might have been only wind. Soon there'll be no mistaking it, her whole belly will hop, quake and ripple. She runs a finger along the lips that the head will burst through. 'What the fuck are you doing?' he mutters.

'Nothing.'

'You're breathing hard.'

'No, I'm not.' She forces herself to count as she breathes slowly in one two three, out one two three.

'I can hear you.'

'No.' She moves to the cold edge and listens motionless, breathing very slowly. He is silent. He has had his say.

She wakes at cockcrow when he gets dressed. She hears the van come, then go. She has stayed in bed through all the flurry of their departure, and so has Chloe. They open the kitchen door to find the *somba* burning with a bright flame, the milk boiled, the baby's napkins dried and folded, the day's eggs brought in from the barn and the table laid with bread and cheese and honey under a cloth.

'Oh, lovely!' cries Bell.

'You see?' Chloe snorts. 'She's sorry.'

'She must have been up all night!' Bell could hug the old woman.

'She was. I heard her.'

'She didn't have to do all this for us!'

Chloe stares and shrugs. 'Why shouldn't she?'

Chloe spends the morning washing and rinsing clothes, Bell taking Sophoula for a walk with the camera. The piles of soft snow were frozen overnight; so were the puddles and the clothes hung out on wires and bare brambles. There are no clouds this morning to block the sun or the faded half-moon, and everywhere they go water trickles and drips and glitters. As they come near the schoolyard Sophoula cringes, pulling at Bell.

'Carry me, Auntie Bella.'

'Why, for heaven's sake?'

'The snow woman's there.'

'It's only snow! It's only a big doll made of snow.'

'It's the wicked witch.' She huddles against Bell. 'She comes alive at night and stares in the window.'

'She does not! Look, she's melted. The poor old thing, she's vanished away.' A heap of pitted snow sits under the pines.

'The moon's melting too, Auntie Bella!'

Sophoula keeps Bell company while she boils the potatoes and fries eggs for the four of them for lunch; Chloe is with the baby in the bedroom. But the child is grizzly and cross now and says she isn't hungry: she doesn't want potato or egg or bread or anything. 'Have a bit of banana?' Bell pleads. One banana is left. Chloe has made them last, feeding them to Sophoula inch by inch and folding the black soft skin over the stump. But no, Sophoula won't. 'I know!' On impulse Bell peels the last banana, flours it and fries it in the pan with the eggs for Sophoula. 'My darling, eat,' she says. The old man trudges in. Lunch is late again. 'Try it? For Auntie? Have some milk with it?'

'Tell a story.'

'Once upon a time,' she slips a spoonful of banana in, 'in a little cottage in the woods –'

Sophoula gags and splutters. The old man stares. 'Eat,' he growls. 'It's good for you.'

'No! Auntie, I don't like it!'

'All right, you don't have to eat it.' Blushing with shame, Bell gobbles the banana herself before Chloe comes.

'There was a banana,' Chloe says when they are peeling
fruit into their empty plates later, and Bell tries to explain.
Sophoula announces smugly that Auntie ate it all up. So as
not to let it go to waste, Bell says, red-faced. 'You know
she has them raw,' Chloe accuses. 'No more bananas!'
Chloe kisses the child's hair. 'Wicked Auntie! Where will I
get my darling some more?'

The old man, groping in his pockets, finds a bag of
peanuts in their shells and presses it into Sophoula's hand.

'Is it *safe* to give her nuts?' Bell wonders aloud. 'They'll
choke the child.'

In silence she rinses the dishes while Chloe shells peanuts
by the *somba*. Abruptly Sophoula hoots and stiffens. Her
back arches. Chloe bangs her, shakes her, shoves her head
forward, and at last a great gush of sour curds and speckles
pours out of her mouth all over her mother.

'Thank God!' Chloe hauls her jumper over her head.
'*Aman*, my poor darling!' she moans, dabbing Sophoula's
white face. 'They're bad, don't ever eat them! Wicked
Pappou!' She pushes the whole bag into the firebox and
slams the iron door. The old man plods to his room.
'There,' she says, 'let them burn. He won't tell Her,' she
mutters at Bell, who has brought a glass of water.
'Thanks. Don't you tell either, or we'll never hear the end
of it.'

It is dark these days before the old man wakes to do the
afternoon milking. The torch he takes into the barn lights
up the ridge of snow at the door. His approach to the house
is a clank and slop of saucepans past the window and a red
point and trail of smoke, his cigarette. This time he dumps
the saucepans caked with dung and hay inside on the
kitchen floor and covers them. 'Who'll strain the milk?' he
says loudly to no one. 'Will you boil it or use it for cheese?'

Sullen with sleep in their doorways, the women exchange looks. He is waiting. Chloe tweaks a curl off her

baby's damp cheek and kisses it.

'Two daughters-in-law!' barks the old man and they all jump. The baby whines.

'Sssh.' Chloe frowns.

'Two daughters-in-law and I do it, do I? I strain the milk! I make the cheese! It's not enough to look after the cows and milk them. I can do the lot!'

The kitchen door slams. Chloe pulls Bell into her room, where they stand listening behind the door as he unlatches the window and clatters the saucepans. Then the front door clangs shut and his boots crunch away.

'He's thrown it out!' Bell mutters.

'*Two daughters-in-law and I do it, do I?*'

'Sssh. He'll hear!'

'Him, hear?'

'Sssh.'

They creep to the kitchen and turn the light on. In the square of yellow it throws outside, Bell can just make out the saucepans on end against the barn wall. The sun never comes there and the snow is still thick, with a pale puddle in it, a cat crouched at the edge, and all around a wide shawl of creamier snow. 'Oh! What a waste,' Bell sighs.

'Who cares?' Chloe looks in a jug. 'Look, there's all this left from this morning.'

'He's right, though.'

'It's Mama's job!'

'But since she's not here.'

'I have two small children I have to do everything for.'

'Yes, I should have done it.'

'You're pregnant!'

'Only five months.' She sits down. 'I need a coffee.'

'No, come on, let's get out of this place before we go mad! We'll take the children to Aunt Magdalini's. Come on.'

At Aunt Magdalini's, the village secretary's wife tells them that the bridges have been declared safe for the time being and that a bus to Thessaloniki will run in the morning. Rowdy in her elation and relief and scorn of Kyria Sophia, who might just as well have waited, Chloe hauls Bell and Aunt Magdalini's three daughters-in-law along the crusted, muddy street to celebrate her release at the *kafeneion*.

Inside its misted windows men are smoking at small tables, watching the soccer on the grey television screen (the only one in the village) or looking on while Grigori's father plays the champion at *tavli*. The men all sit with their elbows on the chair-back and their hands flat on their chests, glancing sidelong from time to time at the table of women drinking orangeade. When Grigori's father wins the game he sends the *kafedji* over with another round, and the women raise the bottles smiling in a salute to him.

Chloe tells joke after joke uproariously and the other three are soon helpless with laughter. 'What are the men staring at?' she asks, gazing round. 'Oh, Bella, it's you!' She swoops and whispers, 'Bella, look how you're sitting.' Startled, Bell looks. 'Bella, your hands!' She has them open over each breast exactly as the men's are, but women never sit like that. She moves them to the slopes of her belly and Chloe giggles and nudges but Bell is too torpid in the smoky heat to be bothered. When the others are ready to go they wake her. The sky is all white stars, frost crackles as they tread. They link arms with Bell in the middle to keep her from a fall. Scarves of mist trail behind them. They drop her at home on the way to Aunt Magdalini's.

Alone in the cold bed, Bell is awake for the first unmistakable tremor of the quickening.

Before daybreak Bell is up to strain the milk – twice carefully through the gauze – and boil it in time for breakfast. Chloe's noisy desperation surges all around her. At last the kisses crushing or missing cheeks and she is away with the children, the old man carrying their bags to the bus, and Bell has the house to herself.

She scrubs the saucepans and puts clean water on to boil. The table is littered with crusts, plates and cups under the yellow bulb that only now she remembers to switch off; she tidies up. She has packing to do as well, letters and lists to write, but that had better wait until Grigori decides whether or not to go with her.

When her saucepans boil she carries them and another of cold water into the lavatory annexe that the old man spent all autumn building and is proud of. In case he tries to come in and wash, she pushes the heavy can of olive oil against the door. There is no light bulb in here yet, only an air vent and a candle stuck on a plate. She leans over to put a match to it and its flame lights her breasts: they are as she has never seen them, white and full, clasped with dark veins like tree roots. Shuddering in the cold, she stands in the *tapsi*, wets and soaps herself urgently, rinses the soap off. Flames go down her in runnels. She is rough all over with goosepimples except for her belly, domed in her hands, warm and smooth like some great egg.

All the water is swilling round her legs in the *tapsi* before she has got all the soap off but she rubs herself dry anyway, pulls on her clean clothes and with a grunt hoists up the *tapsi* and pours all the water into the lavatory bowl. It brïms, then sinks gurgling down in froth and a gust of sweet cold rottenness from the sewer belches up in her face.

Still shuddering, she hugs herself close to the *somba*, propping the iron door open while she crams pine cones in. She sits with her clothes open. Perhaps the baby can see and hear the fire, she thinks: did he see my hands in there, by the light of the candle? They must have made shadows on his red wall.

Here we are in a cold white house with icicles under the eaves and winter has hardly begun, but inside its walls are warm to the touch, full of firelight.

She has a couple of hours before she needs to start cooking lunch, and one full roll of fast film left: she will use them to take her last photographs. Bare interiors of sun and shade and firelight, in which as always she appears absent.

CAFFE VENETO

HER FATHER is there already when Anne comes. She sees him first, smoking under a streetlamp outside the misted windows with their gilt scrawl: *Caffe Veneto*. The seedballs and fingered leaves of a plane tree are touching him with shadows.

'You found it, then,' she calls out. 'Sorry if I'm late. I was held up at rehearsal.' He is holding a bottle wrapped in brown paper. 'Is this a celebration?'

'A Cabernet Sauvignon. Good to see you!'

'Yes. It's been a while. Two months?'

'Or three. Since Easter.'

'That's right. Well. What a strange phone call!' This furtive smile of his is strange as well; and how much he has aged since then. In this light his skin seems to have faded and creased, settled more slackly in the hollows of bones. His eyes are smaller. Even his teeth seem smaller, patched and stained, exposed in his uneasy smiles. This austerity of age, in his of all faces, is at the same time intimidating and pitiable. She wonders if he has seen it himself in mirrors.

'Is this place fit for the Cabernet Sauvignon?' she says. 'We could look for somewhere fancier.'

'No, why? They've only changed the name. I have been here before, I remember now.'

'Student food.'

'I live on it. The spaghetti's good, come on.'

The glass door opens and a laughing group pushes out. The bead curtains rattle. Then two barefooted girls go inside; a warm gust, a smell of coffee and smoke, blow out as visibly as breath. He holds the beads aside for her, and the door open. Lamps hang inside, round and red like upturned glasses of wine. In the blurred light they shed, Anne leads him past crowded stools at the counter to the only table free, a long bench against a wall of theatre posters. Its top is carved like a school desk. Her father sits at her side tracing initials on it with his finger while their order is taken and the table set. Only when he pours the wine does he give her his usual undaunted, boyish smile.

'This whole table to ourselves? Well, cheers.'

'Cheers. A 1975! Napa Valley. Californian? Oh, it's nice.' The wine, plummy and dark, stings and makes her shudder. 'So we *are* celebrating?'

'No.'

'No?'

He shakes his head, lighting another cigarette.

'Is Mum all right?'

'Fine. She's minding the children for your Aunt Sheila. She said to give you her love and talk you into coming back for a coffee.'

'Oh. I only signed out for ten-thirty, though.'

He checks his watch. 'How's College?'

'Great.'

'What was that about a rehearsal?'

'Oh yes. The Drama Club's putting on *The Seagull*. Chekhov? You have to come.'

'Of course. Are you Nina?'

'No, only Masha. Poor dreary Masha in black.'

'Well, we must come.' His voice falters. 'When's it on?'

'In two weeks. I'll look after the tickets. Now tell me,' she smiles and holds up her wine glass, 'what we're *not* celebrating.'

'What if we eat first, talk later.'

'No, now. Come on.'

'Well – my study leave's come through.'

'Well, good! I thought you'd decided to withdraw your application.'

'I had. But I'd have missed out altogether. It was now or never.'

'"It's now or never. My love won't wait." So you'll be going to America after all?'

'That was the idea. Funny you should say that.' He gives a short laugh. 'I've fallen in love.'

'Oh Daddy, again?' Her smile is stiff from the wine. 'Not that I can talk. I have, too.'

'*Have* you? What's his name?'

'I don't know him very well.'

'Don't know his name.'

'Not telling. Not yet. He's – he's married. Separated.'

'That's what they all say, they say.'

'Is it now? Anyway, she's moved to Sydney and he's here.'

'Well. What can I say? So long as you're happy.'

'It has its moments. You?'

'Yes. And no.'

'Do I know this one?'

'No.' He hesitates. 'She's one of my post–grad students. She's doing her thesis on Sylvia Plath. Oh, she's mature age,' he adds quickly. 'She's thirty–nine.'

'Married?'

'Divorced with one daughter. As a matter of fact, she's a student here: Microbiology, I think. The daughter. Jenny.'

She nods. 'You've met the daughter. What's the mother's name?'

'Sandra.' He gulps more wine and wipes his lips with a finger.

'So this is not a celebration because now you wish you weren't going to America.'

'In a way.' He fixes earnest eyes on her. 'You haven't seen your mother all this time, Annie, have you?'

'There's never a moment free. There are extra tutorials when you live in at College. And this play. And essays all –'

'I know.' He breathes out smoke. 'I just wondered. When you didn't come home at the end of first term.'

'Did she complain, did she? But she knew I was going camping!'

'No. All I'm saying really, darling, is that now your mother's going to need all your love and support. Please.'

'She doesn't *know*, does she?'

'No. She doesn't.'

'Well. Good.'

'I may have to tell her.' He bows his head and she sees that his grizzled curls, redder under this lamp, are thinning at the crown. 'This time it's the real thing. I may have to leave your mother.'

'For this – for Sandra?'

'When you meet her, you'll understand.'

'Hang on. Hang on.' Bowls of spaghetti thud into place under their noses. She watches her own hand pick up a fork and coil red hanks round and round it, too disconcerted by his lack of composure to take in what he is saying. 'Why *me*?'

'We've always been close.' He tries to smile. 'Trial run?'

'Oh, so it's all *settled*?'

'Darling, nothing's *settled* yet.'

'It sounds settled to me.'

'Not so.'

He stubs out his cigarette and lights another. Anne bends over her spaghetti. She should eat, being unused to wine. She gulps one hot mouthful, feeling her whole head swill with tears; tears of shock.

'Annie.'

'It's the spaghetti. Hot.'

'Damn,' mutters her father. Two people are seating themselves opposite them at the table, backs to the wall, a boy in a football guernsey and a woman in black suede. As alike as the Mother and Child in an ikon – though he must be eight or nine, Anne thinks – they look at each other with pleased black eyes set widely under round brows in their amber faces. Anne moves the wine glasses to make room and the woman smiles.

'It's the only table left.' Anne shrugs, pushing her plate away. She wipes her nose. 'I won't meet Sandra. How could you suggest it? You should know better.'

'I admit I was hoping, well, at least that you'd be more –'

'Amenable?'

'Just understanding.'

'Oh yes. I under*stand*.'

'Not how I feel. Do you?'

'Why not? I've understood the other times. I've kept your secrets. Commiserated when it was over. Haven't I? What I *don't* understand is why this time my mother would deserve to be left.'

'Darling, you don't leave people because they *deserve* it. Or stay with them, either.'

'If that's true, then no one's ever secure.'

'That's how it is. There's no security.'

'If people were *faith*ful –'

'Yes, in an ideal world, people would all be faithful and all be secure. I agree. Or there'd be no love and so no insecurity.'

'They go together, do they?'

'I'd say so. Wouldn't you?'

'No!' At her tone the woman opposite glances up from her struggle to tuck the boy's napkin round his neck, while he digs into ravioli; full of mournful surprise, her eyes meet Anne's. She thinks we're lovers quarrelling, Anne thinks, and looks away, down at her hands. They have been tearing a hunk of bread into crumbs. She picks some up on a fingertip and eats them.

'When do you have until?' she whispers.

'Not long. America, you mean?'

'Yes. Mum must have been thrilled about that?'

'I haven't told her, Annie.'

'Why not?'

'I can't decide, don't you see?' His hand is crepe-skinned and the bones show, bent round the red glass. He sees her looking and looks too, holding his thick fingers outspread.

'I just can't take it in. When will you tell her?'

He winces. 'Oh, we'll more than likely call the whole thing off.'

'Call America off? Because of Sandra?' He stares at her. 'She – Sandra – must have known all along you were married.'

'Of course. Of course. Sorry. I thought you meant when would I tell your mother about Sandra.'

Maybe I did, Anne thinks. She gulps down the tart red wine, feeling dazed. 'How long have you known her?'

'About six months.'

'Six *months*.'

'Sssh. We've been lovers for two. Three.'

'Since Easter. You can't be sure, then. It's too soon.'

'That's what she says.'

'Well?'

'Just that it isn't true. I do love her. I'm only not a hundred-per-cent sure if she's worth the price. If anyone is, I mean. No, I am sure.'

'You mean, worth what *you* will have to pay.'

'Yes.'

'That's – don't you see that's selfish?'

'In a sense it's selfish, I suppose.'

This is what love does, she thinks. Puts us at the mercy of the other's selfishness. And of our own.

'If you believe in love,' he says, 'you pay the price.'

'Except that Mum will be paying the most. And she's always been faithful to you, in spite of your other women.'

'Doesn't that in itself say something about our marriage?'

'Maybe just about marriage.'

'When you get married –'

'I won't.'

'Let's keep our voices down. What's he like?' He smiles. 'This fellow you're in love with? Not that History tutor, is it? What's his name again?'

'I'm never getting married. Never.'

He shrugs. 'Up to you.'

Already he doesn't care, then. 'You know,' she says, 'if you leave her now she'll feel that her life has been wasted.'

'Her love, perhaps. Not her life. Most love is wasted.'

'Her whole *life*.'

'Past life. Okay. Which is it worse to waste, I wonder? The past or the future?'

'Mum, of course, would be concerned about *her* future.'

'She's still a very attractive woman, darling. She'll find someone else.'

'Will she, though? She hasn't had the practice you've had.' There is a grim silence. She stares at the peeling theatre posters: there is one for *The Seagull*. Her mouth is parched, her throat swollen and furred. 'Besides,' she whimpers, 'she loves *you*. Doesn't that count?'

'Annie,' he sighs, 'we have to be mature about this.'

'Are you being?'

'Do you think love is immature?'

'Not in itself.'

He rubs his greying head. The hair on his chest, she remembers from last summer, is greying too, above and about his nipples. He has a young man's belly. Like a tree in autumn he is withering from the top down. Not since the upheavals of puberty has she been so aware of men, the presence of the male, as now. Is it because she has a lover now? Maybe all women feel like this. And men? I still know next to nothing about love, she thinks: and I'll suffer for it.

'You always said to take love lightly,' she says.

He sighs, breathing smoke out. 'I can't be sure I can even go on hiding my feelings at home.'

'But that's not a reason to leave! That doesn't make sense!'

'Why doesn't it?'

'If you can't hide it, tell her. She probably knows.'

'No, I'd know if she did.'

'She always has before.' He stares at her. 'I never told her. Of course not. She never told me straight out that she

knew. She just – hinted. "I think you're like me," she said
last time. "I let lying dogs sleep," and we laughed. You
didn't take it seriously, so . . . And that's what she's doing
now.'

'Why didn't you ever . . .?' He shrugs.

'Tell you? You *know* why. I didn't tell Mum what you
told me either, did I? You both trusted me. And I would
never have dared, anyway. Why do you think I wanted to
live in at College? Because I was out of my depth at home.'

She sees herself wading for the first time beside the huge
white legs of her mother and father into cold green slabs of
water that tilted high and hurled her off her feet. Screaming, she clutched a hand, a knee, clambered on a slippery
thigh. They carried her back to the sandbank. Lapped in
pale water, she sat there alone wailing while they waded
back in without her, deeper and deeper, until they dis-
appeared.

'Secrecy. Lies. Hints,' her father is saying. 'Why
wouldn't she say, if she knew? I didn't want to hurt her,
that's all.'

'Oh, *what* can I say? Can't you just wait a while? You
can't spring a thing like this on her. At least, give her time.'

'Time! That's just it. I'm afraid Sandra won't wait.'

'Won't wait?'

'Won't wait, I mean, if I go off to America for months
with your mother.'

'Why not?'

'It'd be asking too much of her credulity, she says.'

'But if she loves you?'

'It's faith that she lacks. Not love. Faith and hope.'

'It sounds like she's blackmailing you.' He is silent. This
is what he sometimes suspects. Resentfully, in spite of
himself, he pictures Sandra curled and smug on her bed
reading at this moment, the lamplight around her in
flounces of smoke like a mosquito net; while he fights his
daughter for her sake. 'Blackmailing you,' Anne says.
'She'll wait, if you go alone.'

'You still don't understand.'

'*Tell* me.'

'I can't not take your mother, can I,' he mutters, 'if I'm living at home?'

'You can't mean that you want to take *Sandra* to *America*!'

'Annie, enough now. Please. This is dreadful.'

'You do! You do! How *could* you? You can't *mean* it.'

'Annie, for God's sake.'

'You're my father and I love you. You know that. Maybe more than Mummy. But if you leave her, I'll be on her side. I won't even see you again.' She wonders as she says this if it is true; and if he would care. 'I mean that.'

'*Well!*' He pushes his untouched plate away in turn. The boy opposite pauses to stare curiously from the cold tangles of spaghetti to their faces, and back. 'What shall we talk about now?'

'Nothing. I'll go.' But, as he half-expects, she makes no move to. He fills the glasses, drinks his down, and lights a cigarette.

'Big match tomorrow,' he tosses defiantly across the table.

'Yeah!' The boy grins back at him.

'How do you like your chances?'

'Gunna win!' The boy looks for approval at his mother, who gives him an imploring smile. She has finished her ravioli. 'Great ravioli, Mum,' the boy announces, clearly to please her; and she looks pleased.

'I *fear* for my mother!' Anne shouts. 'I fear for her! How will she bear it?'

'Darling!' Shock makes him spill his wine. With his napkin he stanches the dark puddle, wondering if she can be drunk. After all, she has eaten only the bread. He gapes at her in such evident mute dismay that again she strikes her as boyish, an elderly bad boy, and a spasm of laughter crosses her face. Yes, she is, he decides. Grinning with relief, he throws his arm around her shoulders to pull her to him for a moment and she smells suddenly the drenching sweetness in the armpits of men who smoke. But she draws back from him.

'Gunna win, no worries.'

'I don't know, though,' her father teases. 'You're up against the best team, just about.'

'We aren't, they are! And my dad's playing!'

'Your dad, is he? Go on!'

'He's the captain!'

'Is he now? What's his name?'

Again the boy refers to his mother, then leans forward and whispers it.

'He's your dad? Well, good God!' The woman nods, ruefully, it seems to Anne; the dark eyes glimmer and close. 'You going to be as good as your dad?'

'Better!'

'Going to see him play?'

'Too right!'

'Might see you there.'

'Finish, finish.' His mother nudges him: heads are turning in the red haze. He scoops up his last shreds of ravioli, while her father turns his jovial smile on the mother. 'His dad's a magnificent footballer. One of the greats. And you,' he tells the boy, 'must be very proud.' The boy nods gravely, wiping his chin.

The woman springs up. 'Yes, goodnight.' Her voice shakes and she opens her pale palms in a beseeching gesture. 'We going now.' She stoops to the boy's ear. 'Come on. We going.'

'Oh? Can't I have a gelato?'

'Yes, in a cornet. Please, the bill.' She tugs the waiter's sleeve. But the boy wants to hear more. She wavers, but bends her head, blotting her cheeks with her black lapels, and rushes alone to the counter.

Anne leans forward. 'Your mother wants you.'

A black suede arm is beckoning.

'Yeah, I better go.'

'Well, nice meeting you.' Her father puts out his hand;

the boy's tawny hand is lost in it. Confused, he stands smiling at them, glancing now and then towards his mother until at last he can detach himself and run to her.

'How about that?' Her father sits back. 'Nice kid. If he turns out half the man his dad is!'

'I think she was crying.'

He looks round, but they have gone. 'Sorry?'

'She was crying. That's why she rushed off.'

'Why would she be?'

'I think, because of you. All that about his father.'

'He's a great player. Why shouldn't his kid be proud of him?'

'He takes after her,' Anne says. 'Both honey-coloured.'

'So are we in this light.'

'Dark honey. Like a Byzantine Madonna and Child.'

'I thought they looked Indian.'

'Yes? Or Maori.'

'Maybe.' He considers. 'Or Indonesian.'

'The thing is, they were so happy. A dinner out at the Caffe Veneto. She should have been safe.'

'From?'

'She was hurt. Shamed.'

'Why, though?'

'Who knows? The boy's father may have *done her wrong*. Anything. It's none of our business, that's all.'

'Well, she's not his wife. I've met his wife.'

'My point.'

'Anne, all I did was pay tribute to a marvellous bloody footballer!'

'You overdid it.'

'*Did* I.'

'What right had you to make her cry?'

'How was I to know?'

'*I* knew.'

'Well, *I* didn't, I'm afraid. Sorry.' Stung, he makes a hurt face. 'I see nothing I do or say tonight is going to find favour. Poor me.' His lined eyes meet hers. 'Cast into outer darkness.'

'It's all of a piece, that's all.' She tips her head back to empty her glass, and her face glows under the lamp. 'You can choose not to know you're doing it, but still the damage is done. People suffer. Lives are ruined.'

'*You're* overdoing it.'

'You really don't care.' She gazes in disillusion as he sighs. The impetuosity which all her life she has loved in him is not, after all, boyish. In the light of this evening it is shown up as shallow and rash; even, perhaps, brutal. 'You ride roughshod. You'll always get away with it.'

'All right. I'm a clumsy galoot. That boy's mother's life is ruined. *Mea culpa*.'

'In a small way it does go to show,' she says, and holds out her glass for more, 'that you can make strange errors of judgement. Admit that. May I have some more American wine?'

'Just what I was about to say of you.' He fills her glass. His suddenly amused lips look as if they are bleeding, black from the wine. He watches her turn her glass so that the glow of wine moves on the table. 'Can this be our practical Annie?'

'Why can't it?'

'Burning incense to the Madonna of the Caffe Veneto.'

'She thought we were lovers quarrelling.'

'Did she? She can't have heard much.' He glances round. 'I'll bet she was on your side.'

'Being practical,' she says, 'if that's what's expected, tell me: have your loves ever lasted? Has love ever made you happy for long?'

He takes her hands. 'What has happiness got to do with love? "To love is to suffer," didn't Goethe say? "One is compelled to love, one does not want to."' She shakes her head and pulls free. 'Annie.' But she turns away, one hand folded to hide her face.

He foresees himself at the moment when she will stand on tiptoe to kiss him goodnight holding her by the shoulders and pressing with his closed lips a kiss of finality on her stained lips; holding her away, then, to look in her eyes and compel not only resignation. Consent, absolution, belief. When he sees that she can't move first, he holds the bottle up under the lamp and shakes it. 'All gone,' he pouts. He sniffs it: the dregs have a smell of olives. She looks at him. 'Like a coffee?'

'No, thanks.'

'Sure?'

'No, I'd better get back.'

He glances at his watch. 'Let's go? It's after ten.'

While he pays she droops at his side staring at her shoes on the bare planks, in an attitude of reproach, as he notes wryly. Whatever gave me the idea, he thinks, that I could convince her of the imperatives of love? My shy and scrupulous daughter, of all people! No, her mother's daughter now. He holds her coat open for her to grope into. 'Drive you back to College?'

'I think I'll walk.'

'Walk you back?'

'All right.'

It is clammily cold. They walk on a wide path past shadowy trees holding their few brown leaves still in the mist. A full moon glimmers. His daughter's shoulders are folded in; her hair hangs in two rusty skeins along the line of her nose. At eighteen she is no longer a girl. Prettier now, yes, but shedding her young freshness. She will be late, as fearful of hurt as she is, to come to ripeness. She has a shrouded look, he thinks; her eyes, when for a moment she glances up, seem full of sorrow and foreboding.

'Give my love to Mum,' she says once. 'Tell her I'll ring.'

'I will.'

'You'll come to the play?'

'Of course. You'll see to the tickets?'

'You have to go to America. Don't you?'

'Yes.'

'With Mum or with Sandra.'

'Yes.'

'What's she like?'

'Beautiful.'

'You were my household gods,' she says as if to herself. 'Warm and luminous. One each side of the fire.'

'Oh, Annie.'

'Oh, I grew out of it.'

She has her hands in her pockets and is staring down at heaps of leaves as she shuffles through them, not close enough for an arm round her shoulders to seem unforced. She is exhausted, of course; so is he, barely able to speak. He breathes long trails of smoke out, thinking of Sandra reading; and of Margaret, at home with his sister's children, waiting.

They come round the crescent and the brick hump of her college stands black on the glow of the sky. Under the trees it is deeply dark. She catches a plane leaf as it floats loose: brown on one side, pale with brown veins on the other, like an imploring hand.

'Have a wish?'

'You know.' She looks at him. 'Daddy, you won't do it. Will you?'

'No.' He turns his stubbornly pleading face to her, but she is looking down again. 'No, I don't suppose I can.'

'You mustn't.'

'I won't. No.'

On the gravel at the entrance she turns abruptly and kisses him, her hands on his shoulders, and runs up the steps. Her mouth tastes of tears. I never asked about her love affair, he thinks. He starts back, his shoes crunching in the mist. But she is inside the blurred glass door, which is slowly closing. Her shape stoops, signing in. The light goes out, and the lock clicks.

THE HAREM

WHEN BELL was nine the S.E.C. transferred her father from Melbourne to Wangalla for nine months. In no time he was sick and tired of living in a room at Doolan's pub. He sent Bell and her mother scrawled postcards full of loneliness. For the school holidays he found them a cheap house near the station, and they could have the run of it but for Mr Grey's own front room where he kept himself to himself. Bell sneaked in for a look. His double bed was a smelly bundle of grey sheets and blankets. Morning sunshine burned in fluff all over his oiled floor and the dusty mirror over his dressing table.

Mr Grey owned the house opposite too, where the Harem lived. He owned the woodyard next door, its stacks of red-furred wood guarded by a savage dog. It said so on the gate. He owned half of Grey Bros iceworks; sometimes they met him on hot afternoons, chipping out shimmering blocks and carrying them wrapped in sacking on his shoulder into the shaded houses, while his horse stamped. Mr Grey was a widower and childless, and ought to have been well off but for his drinking problem. Bell thought he was old, but her mother said no, but he'd let himself go. Mr Grey was affable in the evenings and surly before noon. His little wrinkled eyes had veins, and when he yawned he showed yellow pegs of teeth. He spent most afternoons in the pub and even ate there. He shambled in about seven, banging doors, and sometimes crashed and swore, and sometimes sang snatches of 'Knees up, Mother Brown' or 'Oh, you beautiful doll'.

The yard at Mr Grey's was shaded by a red-leafed tree dripping with little red plums sweet and yellow inside and warm when the sun was in them. A tame bird lived behind the tree. A curlew, Mr Grey said. It squatted in the dust or minced around and cocked its gold eyes. Once Mr Grey caught Bell throwing plums at it to make it hop and bridle.

'Know what happens to kids ut do that, do yer?' he growled. 'Bird gets in at night. Pecks their eyes out and swallers um.'

All night in the dark it hovered. A weird cry, a scimitar beak. Her mother insisted on fresh air. Every night once her light was off Bell leapt up and latched her windows.

Down the lane from the house there was a long foot-bridge over the railway lines, and the Spirit of Progress surged under it gushing great clouds and hooting. The wheels pumped, grinding, glittering. The high blue engine whooped. Every morning Bell rushed to the bridge for the Spirit to wrap her in hot white billows.

Once as she tore out she saw that the woodshed gate was open, the red dog bounding up, barking, slavering. She propped, but he only wanted to prance and bow and lick her hands. The Spirit shrieked. Bell and the dog took off and reached the bridge in good time. When the train had slid away they sauntered back together.

'If yer gunna take Rover out,' Mr Grey warned, 'watch out yer bring um back. Worth a packet, that dorg is.'

After that whenever the dog saw Bell he bowed and whined, a slobbery wood-chip in his teeth for her to throw. At Spirit time he jumped at the gate with his tail whipping. She called him Red, not Rover. Red was covered in such tight curls he looked as if June had permed him with her lotions and pins.

June lived with Mr and Mrs Peterson and their daughter Kate in the Harem. Mr Malone the grocer called it that. Met the Harem yet? He winked at Bell's mother but she seemed not to notice.

'Mum, what's a harem?'

'Oh, a sort of Arab family.'

June was tall and heavy, with curly red hair – hennaed, Bell's mother said – as glossy as plum-skins. Advertisements in shop windows said that Miss June Smith did hairdressing in your own home by appointment. Bell's mother said June looked fast, and she was, pedalling along from head to head on a glittering bicycle with netted wheels. Women waited for her with their hair lank and wet in kitchens soaked in the waxen light of hot sun behind holland blinds. Often three or four women would wait in the kitchen of one of them, who laid on tea with buns, or scones, or fruitcake. The teapots wore their best knitted cosies. June's bicycle was parked on all the best Wangalla verandahs. Sometimes it was leaning on the hot brick wall of Doolan's for all the world to see.

When Bell's mother first had her hair done, she hadn't met the other S.E.C. wives, so no one else was there until Mr Grey slouched in. June laughed and smoked and told long jokes, and ate more than her share of the buttered Boston bun at afternoon tea time. When she had gone, Mr Grey wiped crumbs off his whiskers, sighed, and muttered, 'Fine figure of a woman. They say she's got a temper, but. Stands to reason, eh? Hair like that.'

Bell's mother sniffed.

'I reckon it's a blasted waste,' Mr Grey droned on.

Bell and her mother met Mrs Peterson at the grocer's. She had a toothy grin and long hair coiled in a dun roll on the bone of her nape. She was so homesick for the Old Country. Here the neighbours were so standoffish, weren't they? Do call me Mary, she said. Bell's mother said to call her Judith. Well now, how would Judith's little girl like to come over and play with her Kate? Kate wasn't much older really, only eleven, and so awfully lonely, poor child.

Sullenly dressed up in frills and strap shoes Bell was sent

over to play.

Kate was tall and slim with a white face and straight black hair. Bell was tubby and pink, her hair butter-coloured. Kate was allowed to be barefoot, and dressed all in black. She had bitten her scarlet nails. Her eyes when they met Bell's were long and scowling, unsmiling. With her light on in bright daylight she showed Bell her treasures, her jewels, her greasepaints. She was going to be an actress. She let Bell try on in the dressing table mirror her Arabian brass bangles – so they *were* Arabs – and the strings of green and gold glass beads she spent her time threading. She showed Bell fuzzy photos of her relatives back home, then they sat on her bed to read her Enid Blyton books, stealing glances at each other in the yellow glare of the lamp.

When Kate said 'grass' it rhymed with 'mass'. She said 'somethink' and 'anythink', and called lemonade 'pop'. Later Bell's mother was annoyed when she said things Kate's way: don't copy poor speech, Annabel, please.

Bell was asked to stay to dinner, and ran across to ask her mother, who said yes. With the door open, the Peterson's kitchen table only just fitted in between the stove and the ice chest. Mr Peterson squeezed in on one side between Mrs Peterson and June, and Bell and Kate sat opposite. The light bulb was on a cord and swilled shadows over them with every gust of the northerly. The table cloth of pages from the *Age* lifted, flapped. They had a sweetish red stew with lumps of meat and soft potatoes, and drank 'shandies' of beer and lemonade mixed. They all called the lemonade 'pop'. A rare treat for Bell, it was spoilt by the beer. The grown-ups had just beer. Their breaths smelled like the hot buffets of air when the bar doors opened at Doolan's. Bell's parents never touched liquor.

'Coom on, Mary. Drink oop, loov.' Mr Peterson cuddled Mrs Peterson, winking at Bell. But Mrs Peterson only shook her drooping head.

After the stew Bell thought she should say thank you for

the lovely dinner and go home, but Mrs Peterson gave them all peaches and spotty apples from the ice chest. They peeled them on to their dinner plates. June, showing Bell how to cut her apple through its equator to make a star-apple, dropped it and splashed stew on Bell's dress. June peeled her own apple all in one piece and tossed the peel over her shoulder to see who she would marry. Mrs Peterson's bony nose turned red. You couldn't make out any letters in the coils of apple peel. June and Mr Peterson lit cigarettes and blew smoke.

'Cheer oop, Mary, for the loov of Mike,' Mr Peterson boomed. 'Ah'll open anoother bottle. Put a bit of life into the blooming proceedings.'

'I'm making coffee, Bob,' was all Mrs Peterson said, putting the jug on. Their coffee wasn't boiled in a saucepan with grounds on top, but mixed with syrup from a long black bottle with a picture on the label of a turbanned Arab. At home Bell was only allowed a drop of tea or coffee in her milk. She and Kate filled their coffee with sugar. Not even Kate was taking any notice of Bell. They were all shiny with sweat.

After the coffee Mr Peterson and June left the table hand in hand and shut themselves in a bedroom. Mrs Peterson sighed and boiled the jug again for the dishes. Bell helped scrape plates. Footsteps shambling down the back path startled them all. 'The boogie man,' breathed Kate in Bell's ear. But with a cough Mr Grey's shabby head was thrust into the lamplight. He said no thanks to coffee. He'd just dropped in to pass the time of day. He'd better be orf home, thanks, Mary.

When Bell asked Kate in her room what her father and June were doing, Kate said that if she didn't know at her age, thut was too bud, wasn't it? She shrugged.

'Bob looves them both. Me moom and June.'

'Oh.'

'He likes me best. He said so.'

'Oh, really?' was all Bell's mother had to say to that

when she heard.

That was another interesting thing: Kate's father would only answer to 'Bob', not 'Father' or 'Dud'. He wore a bristly brown moustache and once belted Kate with his razor strop, and worked as a foreman at the cannery.

'Mum, can we buy that Arab coffee?'

'No, we can't.'

'But it's lovely!'

'They had no business to give a child coffee. You've got sauce on your dress.'

'June did it. It's stew.'

'Don't answer back.'

'Mum, what's a four man?'

Her parents decided that if she was asked again she was to say thank you, but her tea would be ready at home, and then come straight home. Because we say so, they said when she asked why. But she could still go over and play. She kept quiet about the shandies.

Kate came over the next morning to see if Bell could go for a swim in the river with them. Mr Grey said he'd be in that: too right he would. 'Well, well, well. Here's K-K-K-Katy,' sang Bell's father jovially, and Kate said, 'My name's Kate.' Bell's mother said definitely not, what with snags and currents and tiger snakes in the river. Bell's mother and father were awful. Kate was, too. They all were.

That was the Sunday the roast leg of lamb got blown as it waited on the table for the vegetables to cook. Her mother said the flies had got to it, but Bell could only see little white threads in rows, like specks of fat. Her mother said she wasn't to tell a soul, did she hear, and ran over to the Harem to borrow some meat. Bell and Dad read the Sydney Sunday papers. The hot darkness by the firestove was full of the sweaty smell of the roast. A long time later her mother came back with a tin of Spam, and served it cold with the vegetables. Bell sulked and said it was a blasted waste, but had to eat Spam or starve, while in the woodyard Red tore and gulped the grey leg and lay dreaming afterwards with the bone in his paws. The treacly dripping had to be poured into a hole in the garden, not back into its hole in the speckled wax in the dripping-basin.

Bell's mother told Dad that she had found poor Mary alone and in such a state that she had had to stay and calm her down. They sent Bell out to play while she told him all about it.

'Oh. But there's nothing to *do*.'

'Go on, sticky-beak,' grinned Dad.

There were some very hot days that week. For hours Bell lay and read in nothing but bathing togs on the cool linoleum in the kitchen. She was allowed to spray herself with the hose in the yard, squinting through rainbows and sheets of wet light, water pounding her. Tawny butterflies shook their wings. She swung ropes of glittering water under the tree, where the dry lawn glowed all over with soft plums. Her mother spent one whole afternoon boiling and bottling jam, some for them and some for Mr Grey. At teatime she sighed, saying how in Melbourne they could have just hopped on a bus and been at the beach in no time. She and Dad quarrelled that night in their hot room beyond the wall. Things were scurrying on top of Bell's ceiling. Her mother was always hoping to high heaven it was nothing worse than possums.

At the window the curlew wailed.

Bell was sent over to the Harem with a jar of plum jam. In her yellow room Kate made her shut her eyes. 'Now open them,' Kate said. She had a solid glass egg. When Bell cupped it in her hands like a chicken it was cold and glowed, a heavy drop of stony water, magnifying her palms. Through it she could see all the bulging golden room. A rainbow light lay deep inside. The egg caught lamplight and sunlight and nursed them like seeds.

'It's crystal,' Kate whispered. 'Bob gave it me. It's valuable. I can tell fortunes in it. I can read minds.'

Bell peered again.

'No, it only works for me.'

'How does it work?'

'Never you mind.'

She swore Bell to secrecy. Even so, she hid the egg away and wouldn't say where, or even let Bell have another little look, however much she begged and wheedled.

For a week Bell clung to Kate's side. Every afternoon they walked Red along the river banks or behind the ice cart for chips of ice to suck. Kate showed Bell her school with its empty yard of asphalt and yellow tussocks. Bell showed Kate Mr Grey's curlew. Kate threw plums and one hit it. She wouldn't talk about the crystal egg.

At last, alone in Kate's room while Kate went to the W.C., Bell gave in to temptation. Evening was falling from a hot sky the colour of apricots. In Kate's golden room Bell dared to kneel and go rummaging. But as she grasped it, hard and icy in a singlet in the bottom drawer of the dressing table, Kate's face appeared. It glared down at her in the lit mirror.

'Put it down, you thief!' Kate hissed.

Bell, sick with shock, turned to face Kate's white face. Had Kate read her mind? They were both shaking, both in pyjamas and slippers, as were the grown-ups, it was so hot, out in the kitchen playing a rowdy game of cards with Mr Grey.

'I only wanted a look!'

'Oh did you now? Well, joost for thut, you're never going to see it again. I've a good mind to tell Bob on you.'

'No, Kate, please!'

'He'll belt you till you bleed.'

'I wasn't going to take it! Why *can't* I have a look? Aren't I your friend?'

'No. You're not. Go home, Sneak.'

Bell stared and burned.

'Go on. Before I change me mind. Tell your moom you're a thief. Tell her I'm not her babysitter.'

Shaken with sobs, Bell ran home. No one saw. She latched her windows and got straight into bed to hide in her hot pillow. She pretended to be asleep when her mother looked in, opened a window and switched off the light. Bell latched it again. The slow night passed. Over breakfast the next day she told about the shandies and so was banned from the Harem forever. She brought up her breakfast though, and had to go back to bed. Her mother and father brought her cool drinks, and food that she couldn't face; they read to her, sponged her, took her temperature and worried all day whether to call the doctor. By teatime she felt a lot better. She had scrambled eggs and slept for fourteen hours.

Next morning Kate was out on the footpath with scrawny Cynthia Malone, the grocer's daughter, drawing with chalks, so Bell had to make herself go out for the Spirit, with Red for company, prancing. They whispered and giggled behind her back. Afterwards they were still there having snail races, prodding the frothed brown shells and barracking. Cynthia's baby brother that she was supposed to be minding picked one up and ate it.

The gas heater blew up that afternoon. No one could have a bath. Bell's mother cried. She said it was the last straw. Then she said that the last matinee of the panto at the Tivoli was next Saturday, so they could still see it if Bell wanted to, but only if they went home a week early. Bell was overjoyed. She wanted to go home very badly. Even though it would mean leaving Dad and Red. So that was all settled.

June came over after tea to give Bell's mother's hair a quick trim. She was in a hurry and took puffs of her cigarette as she snipped.

'No time for a coopa, thanks, dear,' she said. 'No rest

for the wicked.'

'June?' Bell said. 'Can Kate really read minds with her crystal egg?'

'Not now, Bell, June's busy.'

'What's thut, Bell? Did Kate tell you she had a crystal egg?'

'She *showed* me. It's beautiful.'

'Well, well. And where does she keep it?'

'In her bottom drawer in a singlet. It's valuable.'

'I'm sure it is. I'd like to see it.'

'Oh, she won't show you. It's a secret.'

'Oh, I think she will.'

June's face was dark, her crimson lips thin and tight. Bell kept quiet, then.

Over the road that night the lights were still on late, all the lights, and there were shouts and doors slammed. Bell was up way past her bedtime helping her mother with the ironing that she'd put off till then in the cool of the night. Dad looked up from his crossword.

'Sounds like the Sheik's got a war on his hands. Might just pop over and help him out. Even up the odds, eh?'

'It's no laughing matter, Alan. It's a disgrace.'

'Who do you back to win? I'll have two bob on June.' He winked. 'Or one? One Bob on June.'

'Oh, Alan, really. That poor little girl, that's all I can say. What hope has she got?'

'Why's Kate a poor little girl?'

'Never you mind. Off you go now, lovey, it's high time you were in bed.'

'Oh, Mu-um.'

Bell lay awake for ages with her door half-open in the dark, listening to squeals and scamperings above; bird cries outside; silence from the Harem. Her parents' light and Mr Grey's were yellow stripes under their doors.

In the morning the Harem was still silent behind its

blinds until, just before the Spirit was due, the front gate slammed. June was out there alone, holding a suitcase and wheeling her bicycle. Her eyes and hair were hidden by her black-veiled hat, but her plummy lips were tight, her head high for the benefit of starers in the gardens and front windows. As she faltered in the dazing sun, Mr Grey appeared in pyjamas in his doorway, padded to the front door, and opened it. Then June came striding over.

'Well, here I am, Tom Grey,' she said. 'If you still want me.'

'Too right I do,' he said, white under his whiskers. So in she came and snibbed the gate, propped up her bicycle, handed her suitcase to Mr Grey still sagging in the doorway in his fluffed pyjamas, and kissed him. Bell and her mother stood by open-mouthed as Mr Grey and June, hand in hand, shut themselves in his bedroom.

Bell hung around as long as she could, until the Spirit hooted: there were only a few mornings left. That was the golden day they had sandwiches and cordial on a bank of the river where ruffled branches hung their shadows looping in brown water. Red capered then snoozed. Her mother let her take snaps with the Box Brownie, and asked if she was sorry to go and if she'd miss Kate. When Bell said she'd never really liked Kate, her mother nodded, and left it at that.

At teatime they went out for a fish-and-chip tea at the Bridge Cafe, for the first time ever, to give the lovebirds a go.

'How's that for calling a bloke's bluff, eh?' Dad couldn't get over it. 'Well, he's bitten off more than *he* can chew. What a woman!'

'Can I ask June for a ride on her bike?'

'No, you can't. Don't talk with your mouth full.'

'Must've really done her block to walk out,' Dad went on. 'What set her off, I wonder? That's redheads for you.'

'It's dyed.'

Dad went on about how the blokes at work would be all

agog, especially the ones that drank at Doolan's and had seen it coming. Her mother's answers were in such long words, Bell lost the thread, watching how the white bubbles heaved in a milk shake when you blew down the straw. Her father paid the bill and slipped some pennies in Bell's pocket. They all strolled home arm in arm the long way as the sky turned green and stars showed.

The next few days were a flurry of washing and pegging out wrung sheets and shirts that flapped like yacht sails on the lines; packing suitcases; having goodbye cups of tea in waxy kitchens. Bell and her mother were booked on the Spirit, and Dad was moving back to Doolan's pub. The bicycle stayed proudly on the verandah, but June and Mr Grey never seemed to be in. No one saw Kate or her parents at all, but Mr Grey told Dad that Bob and Kate were moving to Sydney and Mrs Peterson was on her way back to the Old Country. He wrote down Bell's Melbourne address for the wedding invitation.

The day before they went Bell said goodbye to all the house and the yard, the glowing shaggy plum tree stripped of its plums, the ruffled curlew, and poor sad Red who sensed it and whined, thrusting his rough head into her hands. In the house she visited every corner, remembering moments. No one was home. Her heart thumping, she pushed open the door of Mr Grey's front room. His bed was flat now. Silver brushes and combs and bottles of green-gold scent stood on lace on his dressing table. The mirror, burning, reflected Bell's joy and amazement. There at last was the crystal egg. It was glowing with inner fire among the ornaments.

A WOMAN WITH BLACK HAIR

HER FRONT door locks, but not her back door. Like the doors on many houses in her suburb, they are panelled and stained old pine ones, doors solid enough for a fortress: but the back one opens with a push straight into her wooden kitchen. Moonlight coats in icy shapes and shadows the floor and walls which I know to be golden pine, knotted and scuffed, having seen them in sunlight and cloudlight as often as I have needed to; having seen them lamplit too, cut into small gold pictures by the wooden frames of the window, thirty small panes, while I stood unseen on the back verandah. (The lampshades are lacy baskets and sway in draughts, rocking the room as if it were a ship's cabin and the light off waves at sunset or sunrise washed lacily inside it. Trails like smoke wavering their shadows over the ceiling are not smoke, but cobwebs blowing loose.) These autumn nights she has a log fire burning, and another in her front room just beyond. With the lights all off, the embers shine like glass. They fill the house all night with a warm breath of fire.

An old clock over the kitchen fire chimes the hours. One. Two.

Off the passage from her front room is a wooden staircase. Her two small daughters sleep upstairs, soundly all night. Beyond the staircase a thick door is left half-open: this is her room. In its white walls the three thin windows are slits of green light by day, their curtains of red velvet drawn apart like lips. There is a fireplace, never used; hardly any furniture. A worn rug, one cane armchair, a

53

desk with a lamp stooped over books and papers (children's essays and poems drawn over in coloured pencil, marked in red ink); old books on dark shelves; a bed with a puffed red quilt where she sleeps. Alone, her hair lying in black ripples on the pillow.

For me a woman has to have black hair.

This one's hair is long and she is richly fleshed, the colour of warm milk with honey. Her eyes are thick-lidded: I have never been sure what colour they are. (She is mostly reading when I can watch her.) They seem now pale, now dark, as if they changed like water. On fine mornings she lies and reads the paper on the cane sofa under her shaggy green grapevine. She is out a lot during the day. She and the children eat dinner by the kitchen fire – her glass of wine glitters and throws red reflections – and then watch television for an hour or two in the front room. After the children go up to bed, she sits on and reads until long past midnight, the lamplight shifting over her. Some evenings visitors come – couples, the children's father – but no one stays the night. And she has a dog: an aged blond labrador, half-blind, that grins and dribbles when it hears me coming and nuzzles for the steak I bring. It has lolloped after me in and around the house, its tail sweeping and its nails clicking on the boards. It spends the night on the back verandah, snoring and farting in its sleep.

The little girls – I think the smaller is five or six, the other not more than two years older – have blond hair tied high in a sheaf, like pampas grass. (The father is also blond.)

Tonight, though the moon is nearly full, it is misted over. I may not even really need the black silk balaclava, stitched in red, that I bought for these visits, though I am wearing it anyway, since it has become part of the ritual. I am stripped to a slit black tracksuit – slit, because it had no fly – from which I unpicked all the labels. I have the knife safe in its sheath, and my regular tracksuit folded in my haversack ready for my morning jog when I leave the house.

Tonight when the clock chimed one she turned all the lights out. When it chimed two I came in, sat by the breathing fire, and waited. There is no hurry. I nibble one by one the small brown grapes I picked, throwing the skins and the wet pips into its flames of glass, making them hiss. Nothing moves in the house.

When the clock chimes three I creep into her room – one curtain is half-open, as it always has been – to stand watching the puddle of dimness that is her pillow; the dark hair over it.

I saw her once out in the sun untangling her wet hair with her fingers. It flowed over her face and over her naked shoulders like heavy dark water over sandstone. The grass around her was all shafts of green light, each leaf of clover held light. There were clambering bees.

There is a creek a couple of streets down the hill from here. I wish I could take her there. It reminds me of a creek I used to fish in when I was a boy. There were round speckled rocks swathed with green-yellow silky weed, like so many wet blond heads combed by the fingers of the water. (My hair was – is still – blond.) I used to wish I could live a water life and leave my human one: I would live in the creek and be speckled, weedy-haired, never coming out except in rain. I lay on the bank in spools and flutters of water light. A maternal ant dragged a seed over my foot; a dragon-fly hung in the blurred air; a small dusty lizard propped, tilted its head to take me in, and hid in the grass under my shadow.

Over the weeks since I found this woman I have given her hints, clues, signs that she has been chosen. First I took her white nightgown – old ivory satin, not white, but paler than her skin – and pulled it on and lay in her bed one day. It smelled of hair and roses. I left it torn at the seams on the sofa under the grapevine that shades her back verandah. I suppose she found it that night and was puzzled, perhaps alarmed, but thought the dog had done it; anyone might think so. Another day I left an ivory rose, edged with red, in a bowl on her kitchen table. She picked it up, surprised, and put it in a glass of water. She accused her daughters of picking it, I could tell from where I was standing by the kitchen window (though of course what she was saying was inaudible), and they shook their heads. Their denials made her angry; the older girl burst into loud sobs. Another frilled rose was waiting on the pillow in the room with the three red-lipped windows. I wonder what she made of that. They looked as if they were crumpled up then dipped in blood.

I drop a hint now: I sit down in the cane armchair, which creaks, and utter a soft sigh. Her breathing stops. She is transfixed. When it starts again, it is almost as slow as it was when she was asleep, but deeper: in spite of her efforts, harsher. Her heart shudders. For long minutes I take care not to let my breathing overlap hers; I keep to her rhythm. She does not dare to stop breathing for a moment to listen, warning whoever is there, if anyone is, that she is awake. And at last – the kitchen clock chimes four – she starts to fall asleep again, having made herself believe what she must believe. There is no one there, the noise was outside, it was a dream, she is only being silly.

I make the chair creak again.

She breathes sharply, softly now, and with a moan as if in her sleep – this is how she hopes to deceive whoever is there, because someone is, someone *is* – she turns slowly over to lie and face the chair. Her eyes are all shadow. Certainly she opens them now, staring until they water, those eyes the colours of water. But I am too deep in the dark for her to see me: too far from the grey glow at the only tall window with its curtains left apart.

This time it takes longer for her to convince herself that there is nothing here to be afraid of. I wait until I hear her breathing slow down. Then, as lightly as the drizzle that is just starting to hiss in the tree by her window, I let her hear me breathing faster.

'Who is it?' she whispers. They all whisper.

'Quiet.' I kneel by her head with the grey knife out.

'Please.'

'Quiet.'

The clock chimes. We both jump like rabbits. One. Two. Three. Four. Five. I hold the knife to her throat and watch her eyes sink and her mouth gape open. Terror makes her face a skull. 'Going to keep quiet?' I whisper, and she makes a clicking in her throat and nods a little, as much as she dares to move. 'Yes or no?'

She clicks.

'It's sharp. Watch this.' I slice off a lock of her black hair and stuff it in my pocket. 'Well?'

Click.

'*Well?*'

'Yesss.'

When I hold her head clear of the quilt by her hair and stroke the knife down the side of her throat, black drops swell along the line it makes, like buds on a twig.

'Good. We wouldn't want to wake the girls up, would we?' I say. I let that sink in, let her imagine those two little girls running in moonlit gowns to snap on the light in the doorway. Then I say their names. That really makes the pulse thump in her throat. 'They *won't* wake up, will they?'

'No,' she whispers.

'*Good.*'

I press my lips on hers. My mouth tastes of the grapes I ate by her still fire, both our mouths slither and taste of the brown sweet grapes. I keep my tight grip of my knife and her hair. She has to stay humble. I am still the master.

'I love you,' I say. Her tongue touches mine. 'I want you.' Terror stiffens and swells in her at that. 'Say it,' I say.

'I – love you,' she whispers. I wait. 'I – want you.'

Now there is not another minute to wait. I throw the quilt off and lift her nightgown. She moves her heavy thighs and the slit nest above them of curled black hair.

There is a hot smell of roses and summer grasses. I lie on top of her. 'Put it in,' I say, and she slips me in as a child's mouth takes the nipple. 'Move,' I say. She makes a jerky thrust. 'No, no. Make it nice.' Her eyes twitch; panting, she rocks and sways under me.

I have to close her labouring mouth with my hand now; in case the knife at her throat slips, I put it by her head on the pillow (its steel not cold, as hot as we are), and it makes a smear where the frilled rose was. Her nightgown tears over her breasts, black strands of her hair scrawl in red over the smooth mounds of them, warm wet breasts that I drink. Is this the nightgown? Yes. Yes. Then we are throbbing and convulsing and our blood beats like waves crashing on waves.

None of these women ever says to me, How is your little grub enjoying itself? Is it in yet? Are you sure? Can it feel anything? Oh, well, that's all right. Mind if I go back to sleep now? No, move, I say, and they move. Move nicely. Now keep still. And they do.

'Now keep still,' I say, picking up the knife again. She lies rigid. The clatter of the first train tells me it is time. Day is breaking. Already the grey light in the window is too strong to be still moonlight, and the dark tree has started to shrink, though not yet to be green and brown. 'I have to go. I'll come again,' I say as I get up. She nods. 'You want me to. Don't you.' She nods, her eyes on the hand with the knife.

I never will. I never do. Once is all I want. At night she will lie awake thinking I will come to her again. Just as she thinks I might cut her throat and not just slit the skin; and so I might. But their death is not part of the ritual. The knife is like a lion-tamer's whip: the threat is enough. Of course if the threat fails, I will have to kill her. She, for that matter, would turn the knife on me if she could. Chance would then make her a killer. Chance, which has made me the man I am, might yet make me a killer: I squat stroking the knife.

'Well, say it,' I say.

'Yes.'

'You won't call the police.' She shakes her head. 'Or will you? Of course you will.' My smile cracks a glaze of blood and spittle around my mouth. In the grey mass on the pillow I watch her eyes roll, bloodshot, bruised, still colourless. 'I want you to wait, though. I know: wait till the bird hits the window.' A bird flies at her window every morning. I see her realize that I even know that; I see her thinking, Oh God, what doesn't he know? 'That's if you love your little girls.' Her eyes writhe. 'You do, don't you. Anyone would.' Girls with hair like pampas grass. 'So you will wait, won't you.' She nods. 'Well?'

'Yes.'

Her coils of dark hair are ropy with her sweat and her red slobber, and so is her torn gown, the torn ivory gown that I put on once, that she never even bothered to mend. A puddle of yellow haloes her on the sheet. She is nothing but a cringing sack of stained skin, this black-haired woman who for weeks has been an idol that I worshipped, my life's centre. The knowledge that I have got of her just sickens me now. Let them get a good look at what their mother really is – what women all are – today when they come running down to breakfast, her little girls in their sunlit gowns. 'You slut,' I say, and rip her rags off her. 'You foul slut.' Just having to gag her, turn her and tie her wrists behind her and then tie her ankles together makes me want to retch aloud. Having to touch her. But I stop myself. Turning her over to face the wall, I pull the quilt up over the nakedness and the stink of her. I wipe my face and hands, drop the knife and the balaclava into my haversack, and get dressed quickly.

The dark rooms smell of ash. Light glows in their panes, red glass in their fireplaces. The heavy door closes with a jolt. I break off a bunch of brown grapes with the gloss of the rain still on them. The dog snuffles. Blinking one eye, it bats its sleepy tail once or twice on the verandah.

I have made a study of how to lose myself in these hushed suburban mornings. (The drizzle stopped long ago. Now a loose mist is rising in tufts, and the rolled clouds are bright-rimmed.) I am as much at home in her suburb as I am in her house, or in my own for that matter, though I will never go near the house or the suburb, or the woman, again. (I will find other women in other houses and suburbs when the time comes. Move, I will say, and they will move. Move nicely. They will. Keep still. Then they will keep still.) And when the sirens whoop out, as of course they will soon, I will be out of the way. I will wash myself clean.

I am a solitary jogger over yellow leaves on the echoing footpaths. No one sees me. I cram the grapes in my haversack for later.

I know that soon after sunrise every morning a small brown bird dashes itself like brown bunched grapes, like clodded earth, at the bare window of her room, the one with its red curtains agape. Again and again it launches itself from a twig that is still shaking when the bird has fallen into the long dry grass and is panting there unseen, gathering its strength for another dash. (The garden slopes away under her room: no one can stand and look in at her window.) It thuds in a brown flurry on to its own image shaken in the glass. It startled me, in the garden the first morning. I think of her half-waking, those other mornings, thinking, It's the bird, as the brown mass thudded and fell and fluttered up to clutch at the twig again: thinking, Only the bird, and turning over slowly into her safe sleep.

But she is awake this morning. She is awake thinking, Oh God, the bird, when will the bird? Twisting to free her hands and turn over: Please, the bird. Her shoulders and her breasts and throat are all ravelled with red lace. Her hair falling over them is like dark water.

MARKET DAY

THE MARKET town stayed green even now, when the fields of ripe wheat and barley all around for mile after mile were scorched and the simmering air wavered in ripples over them. The stork, its long legs trailing back like a mosquito's, dipped over its frayed shadow, landing to prod the stubble. Over fields and cracked creek beds the crows flapped: ka ka ka ka-o.

But the market town stayed green. Everywhere leaves dripped over mossy stone and the carved wood of balconies, and the sound that underlay all other sounds there even in midsummer was the sound of water moving. Mikri Elpida had noticed that about the market town even as a child who could see. Now that she was blind, it was what she loved most. On every market day that the family went she insisted on going, jolting and stifled in the bus from the village. Even then there were all the sounds of water, even on market days, when the *pazari* drew in the buses roaring from every village, honking and farting; and tractors and motor *trikykla*, trucks and cars and horses-and-carts all crowded in; and felted donkeys minced along the damp streets between tiers of tomatoes, peppers, peaches packed in boxes. It was always the same. Then, as now, ragged women offered their crumbles of white butter folded in leaves. In the laneway, where whiffs of coffee and cumin and charring *souvlakia* caught at you as you passed, rows of plucked chickens hung their red necks out of windows. Soldiers and priests, gentlemen in suits, gypsies and grim little pigtailed widows pattered past, as they

61

always had. Jostling strangers pounced, called your name and turned out to be relatives, all with some thrilling piece of news to tell.

When you were tired, you found a table outside one of the three *kafeneia* under the plane trees of the Square, as near to the spilling, rippling fountain as you could, and revived over a coffee, an ouzo with salty *mezedes* to eat, a cold *limonada*. It was the same, year in year out, season by season. When it snowed you sat inside round the stove. The mountain thawed and all the street gutters swelled with ringing tunnels of glass, and soon the Square was overhung with wisteria in bunches. In midsummer all the great plane trees dropped darkness over the tables and the fountain, over your lifted face.

Mikri Elpida always took her knitting, for company, she said: and she was glad of it today. Her brother's daughter, Nitsa, sipping her *limonada* opposite was sunk in silence. Nitsa's silences were new these summer holidays, no one knew why. Her mother, Megali Elpida, had dumped her with Mikri Elpida and dragged the rest of the family off to carry shopping. Click click, chattered Mikri Elpida's needles. In the family, jokes – worn thin now – were still made sometimes about their names. Big Hope and Little Hope: just because Mikri Elpida's brother had happened to marry another, taller and slightly older, Elpida, and since they all lived in the one house . . . But Big Hope, Little Hope! People had to smile. Little hope indeed, for a blind girl with no dowry! Still, you never knew. Elpida smiled. Click click, click click. The wool tickled her cool hands.

'You're like a knitting machine,' Nitsa whined.

Elpida's hands clenched. 'I always knit. I'm sorry.'

'No – you're so good at it, that's what I mean.' Nitsa's voice warmed, by way of apology. Poor Aunt Elpida. But life was so cruel! Always alone, yet never alone for a moment! And must men keep staring like that? Those soldiers by the fountain . . . She had an impulse to tell

Elpida her secret. What would Elpida know about love, though? She was like a quail in a cage. A dry little nun.

'You can knit just as well!' trilled Elpida. Hadn't she herself taught Nitsa? 'Don't you flatter me, now!' Nitsa, with a peevish shrug, decided: no. And now two of the soldiers were strolling over. Elpida went on laughing. Even her laugh was birdlike, in shrill staccato chirps. We must look like two schoolgirls, she was thinking, to anyone who doesn't know us. Maybe not *school*girls, no. Besides, wasn't Nitsa a full-bodied woman now? She had been for two summers: since she was – yes, fourteen . . .

Just then the two soldiers, as if they had every right, scraped back chairs at their table, and one said hotly, boldly, in Mikri Elpida's ear, 'You don't mind if we sit with you, do you, Yiayia?'

'Yiayia?' Did they take her for Nitsa's grandmother? 'Yiayia? Me? Imagine!' tinkled Elpida. Nobody heard. The soldiers and Nitsa were all suddenly talking at once: Nitsa was furious. The soldiers shambled off, Nitsa's shout of 'Who do you think you are?' lashing their backs.

'Imagine! He called me Yiayia,' Elpida persisted.

Nitsa snorted. 'They've got a nerve! Soldier boys! No, thank you!' She sucked on her straw. And burning behind her dark glasses, Elpida knitted.

A grandmother? Nitsa smiled. She looked nothing like one; just like a little brown aunt. She was thin, she was agile and sprightly. With her plaits and her always eagerly tilted face, she looked young: until you saw that the face had set as heavy as clay behind the black glasses, and the hair under the crown of plaits was grey. When she dried it in the sun, the bronze cape of it swept close to the ground. But down to her armpits it made a grey veil. 'Your plaits look as if you knitted them on,' Nitsa remarked.

'Really, do they?'

'Yes, a thick grey and brown knitted cap. If I bought the wool, what if you knitted me a pullover? Would you? Those exact colours, I think.'

Mikri Elpida was open-mouthed.

'Oh, not for me.' Nitsa hesitated. 'Listen – can you keep a secret?'

Grey! A thick grey and brown knitted cap! Worse, worse than being called Yiayia! Elpida's lips shook. Of course, there had to be some grey in it by now, but –

'*How* grey?' she burst out.

'. . . What? Oh, well, not at the ends, only on top. It's like the rings of a tree, isn't it? You can read your whole life in it. If I buy the wool, will you knit me a thick pullover? Will you? Say yes.'

'We'll see.' Elpida's lips were stiff now. No one had ever told her. She was a grey Yiayia, she who had hardly lived. She was a knitting machine.

Megali Elpida pounced on them then and bore them off to the hospital on the leafy hill, where an old aunt from another village had recently had a gangrenous leg amputated. The corridors and the wards breathed ether and phenol, sweat and hot linoleum. Eyes everywhere tracked them past. Megali and Mikri Elpida sat on Aunt Lena's bed, holding a papery hand each. Nitsa, discomforted, took the peaches they had brought over to the washbasin and rinsed them until their velvet skins darkened. The ward filled with the rosy smell of peaches. Now and then Aunt Lena muttered, clutching the hands to her cheeks, 'Ach, Elpida! Elpida!' That there was no hope all of them knew. Tears seeped down their faces.

Out in the sun, rowdy as children let out of school, they marched down arm-in-arm to sit by the fountain again and drink cold ouzo and savour the strong *mezedes* fiercely: the black bitterness of olives, sour peppered cheese with a green gloss of oil, hair-boned anchovies crusted with salt. Before they could finish, the family swooped and rushed them staggering off to catch the last bus. Bags of shopping punched their knees. Hoisted up by the elbows, stifling her gasps, Elpida stumbled along. *Bouzoukia* jangled. In the smoky oven of their bus – nobody would hear of opening a window – she fell asleep on Nitsa's shoulder, her stitches dropping, and woke only when the bus braked in its own dust at the village stop.

Oozing dusty sweat, Elpida said she was tired and went straight upstairs to lie down. In the kitchen, meatballs began to sputter in hot oil. The hens in the yard squabbled. Then the sun slid away and water was pounding into the bucket: the tired cow came clattering home. Elpida unplaited her hot hair. You can read your whole life in it! Your wasted life. I won't go to the *pazari* again, she decided. Never. Never. Coolness flowed in at the window. A cat wailed.

At nightfall the cats, sprawled moth-eaten furs all day, came alive and squatted outside to stab their green gaze at beetles and moths and mice. All the family sat in a circle in the yard, with only the kitchen light on, and the radio, though nobody listened. Neighbours and relatives strolling along the road were called over. Megali Elpida and Nitsa brought out plate after plate of meatballs, fried potatoes, bread. Our kitchen is a lantern in the dark, Nitsa thought, dropping crumbs for the cats: everyone gathers like moths outside it. Everyone, she saw, except Mikri Elpida – who more than anyone loved to sit outside in the dark.

'Where's my aunt?' she asked Megali Elpida.

'Lying down. Let her rest.'

Knocking, Nitsa swept in without waiting to be told. Mikri Elpida was huddled by the window, her loose hair pooling in her lap. 'Who? No!' Her voice quavered. 'Leave the light off!'

'Why are you up here by yourself?'

'I have a headache.'

'Oh, me too!' Nitsa flopped on the bed. 'It's the *pazari*. The heat.' Against the light thrown up from the yard, Elpida was a draped bronze statuette. Nitsa told her so. The answer was like a sob. 'Don't *cry*!' she protested, going nearer. But you never knew when Elpida was crying, even when you could see her eyes. They always looked tightly squeezed; no white edge showed. 'You *are* crying, aren't you? What's wrong?'

'Nothing!'

'Then come down. Come on.'

'Later.'

'What's *wrong*?'

'*Aman*, Nitsa. Don't be such a baby.'

Nitsa dipped her hand under the hair to press it to her aunt's forehead. 'Is the pain there?'

'No, in my heart,' Elpida muttered unexpectedly; straight away her face burned Nitsa's palm.

'Ach, me too,' Nitsa crooned. 'Where's your brush?' She pulled the brush through rustling handfuls of Elpida's spilt hair. 'Isn't it sad how cruel life is?'

'How would you know?'

'Everyone knows.'

Which might be so, for all Elpida knew.

'Is it Aunt Lena?'

'Oh, everything.'

'Because of your eyes too?' murmured Nitsa.

'It's my own business.'

'You can tell me, I won't tell.'

'Well, my eyes, I suppose. In a way. Yes.'

'Do you remember when you could see?'

'Of course. I'm not so old . . . I see dreams every night.'

'Tell me how it happened.'

'But I have.' Everyone knew the story.

'Again.'

'All right. We children had climbed that red hill above the road into town, where everyone's grapevines were. Some of those old vines are still bearing, they're hidden behind the fig trees.' Her hair crackled round her as Nitsa brushed. 'Our mothers had given us baskets to pick the figs and grapes. I remember figs that the birds had torn open, hanging down like thick purple flowers, the seeds spilling. Heavy rains had washed tree roots out and made

66

gullies full of red mud. Saki found a smooth shape buried in one. It looked like glass. "Treasure!" he shouted. Yordani found a mattock and we all crowded round. Then the mud erupted, we were thrown down. That's all I remember. When I dream about it, that's how it ends: a blaze of noise and when I wake up – I can't see.'

Nitsa hugged her. 'It was a German shell,' she prompted.

'. . . A live German shell. There are still some left, people say. Six of us were injured. Saki and Yordani died, torn open like the ripe figs . . . I remember when I could see, but times change. So I can't be sure of knowing what anything looks like now, I suppose.' She swung her hair. 'Today, by the fountain –'

Nitsa stopped brushing. 'What do you think *I* look like?'

'Like a – silly, how would I know?'

'Am I pretty?'

'Well, are you?'

'I know someone who thinks so!'

'What's this?'

'You won't tell, if I tell you a secret?' she whispered. 'Well – I'm in love.'

'Don't *tell* me!' Elpida jumped up. 'And I *thought* maybe – by the fountain today – a thick pullover! *Oh yes*, I thought. *It's for a man*,' and instantly she was sure she had thought that by the fountain.

'So can we buy the wool at the next *pazari*?'

'Slow, slow. Who is he? Do we know him?'

'You won't tell?'

'Never.'

'Well, his name's Aleko. He lives in Thessaloniki and he's a student.'

'And is he in love with you?'

Nitsa giggled. *'Madly!'*

'So life's *cruel*, is it?' scoffed Elpida.

'But I can't see him, can I? Not for weeks! I'll be stuck here in a village all summer till school starts and he's in Thessaloniki!'

'You'll work something out. What if – could he come to our *pazari*, do you think?'

'Yes!' Nitsa hugged her. 'Will you help us?'

'How?'

'To be alone together for a while?'

'You be sensible! You hear?'

'I will, I will. Now come down and eat. Please?'

'My hair!' protested Elpida.

'*Nitsa*, are you upstairs? *Nitsa!*' shouted Megali Elpida from the yard.

'Now what?' Nitsa leaned out. 'Coming!' She sighed. ' "*Nitsa, Nitsa,*" ' Elpida's fingers were twitching in and out of her dim skeins of hair. 'Tomorrow,' Nitsa said, 'I want you to plait my hair like that.'

'You can do it. It's easy.'

'It isn't. I can't.'

'We'll make a thick black cap of it, will we?'

'Not as thick as yours.'

'Flattering me again! Go on down, I won't be long.'

'Let me get you something to eat. Meatballs? Salad? All right?'

Elpida bit back her usual proud rejection of help. 'All right,' she said.

'Remember – it's our secret!' Nitsa flung the door open, clattered downstairs. Elpida sighed. Market day certainly tired you out. But how exciting! What a thrilling piece of news! Tubby, wilful little Nitsa – a fine sweet woman she was turning out, and in what seemed no time at all! Yet wasn't it a little shocking? In love, already! Aleko. Was he handsome, young, brilliant? He must be. He loved Nitsa – *madly*. Remember, our secret. How mystified everyone would be when they saw her knitting, the same as always, a thick pullover – for no one knew who! For Aleko. She would sit in the dark of the plane trees, the water beside her bubbling, brimming over – she remembered how the water looked – with splashed shadows of leaves and clouds. People might even think *she* was the one . . . Mikri

Elpida's laugh trilled out. Voices answered. Dancing with impatience in the doorway, she pinned up her bronze crown.

HOME TIME

BY LATE afternoon the sky is a deep funnel of wind, damp and white. She remarks as she passes through the lamplight around his desk on her way to the bathroom: 'Doesn't it look like snow!'

'Do you think?' He squints out the window.

'That hollowness of the light.'

'It's early for snow.'

'*Casablanca*'s going to be on TV tonight at eight,' she says before he can look down again. 'Why don't we go to that bar and see it and then have dinner somewhere after?'

'Mmm.'

The room is grey; only the light around him is warm and moving with shadows. The steam pipes are silent. Whenever will they start clanking and hissing and defrost the apartment? '*Isn't* it cold, though!' she says brightly.

'Mmm.'

'Maybe I should go for a walk downtown, take some photos of the lights coming on,' she says.

'It's a lot colder outside.'

'Walking would warm me up.'

'Okay.'

'Oh, maybe not,' she says. 'I might write letters home instead.' Home is Australia. It's summer there. 'Until it's time for *Casablanca*.'

He sighs and waits for silence.

She has an electric radiator on in her room – the sitting-room really, but she works in here. She has twin lamps of frilly glass at twin tall windows inside which wasps sizzle

71

and cling and trap themselves in shreds of cobweb. The table she writes at faces the windows. Three times a day she pushes books to one side and turns papers face down, since this is also the table they eat at. The kitchen is next to it, bare and icy, smelling of gas. She pulls her radiator over by the couch and lies curled up in the red glow with her head on a velvet cushion.

Later she half-wakes: he has walked past into the kitchen. When he switches her lamps on and hands her a mug of coffee she is stiffly sitting up to make room. 'Did you get much written?' She yawns, stretching an arm warm with sleep along his shoulders.

'Fair bit.' He grins. 'Did you?'

She is glad she stayed in. 'No. What's the time?'

'Hell, yes.' He looks. 'Ten past eight.'

'Oh, we've missed it!'

'No, we haven't. Only the start.'

They gulp their coffee and help each other drag coats and boots on. 'You must have seen it, haven't you?' he says.

'Oh, yes. Hasn't everyone?'

'Then what's the – ?'

She shuts his mouth with a kiss. 'I want to see it with *you*. In America.'

He smiles at that. They fling open the door and stop short. Snow is falling, must have been falling for hours, heavy and slow, whirling round the white streetlamps. 'Oh, *snow*!' She dashes back inside for her camera and takes photo after photo from the stoop, of fir branches shouldering slabs of snow, drooping in gardens, and elms still with gold leaves and a fine white skin all over, and lawns and cars and rooftops thickly fleeced. Passing cars have drawn zips on the white road.

'Now we're really late,' he says. Hand in hand they tramp and slither the few blocks to the bar they like, bright as a fire with the lamps on. Outside it two young men are throwing snowballs. She gasps as one leaps on the other and they flounder giggling at her feet.

'Pussy cat!' one jeers. 'That's *all* you is!'

Her man is holding the blurred glass door open. Heads along the bar turn away from *Casablanca* to stare at them. He leads her to a stool, orders a red wine and an Irish coffee and stands at her back. Ingrid Bergman's face fills the screen.

The door opens on a white flurry and the young men stamping in, shaking the snow off. The heads turn and stare. 'Celebrate the first *snow*!' one young man announces. 'Have a *drink*, everybuddy!' A cheer goes up. The barman brings her another red wine and him another Irish coffee. The young men have flopped crosslegged on the carpet and are gazing at the screen.

'Oh, they're *so* young,' a voice murmurs in her ear; the grey-haired woman beside her is smiling. She smiles in answer and gives herself over to *Casablanca*. He is at her back with his arms round her. When it ends he goes to the men's room.

The old woman is dabbing her eyes. 'Oh dear!' She makes a face. 'Do you come here a lot? I do. We live just down the road.'

Do you come here a lot? I do. We live just down the road. You can see this bar from our stoop and I tell you it's a real temptation, glowing away down here. With that lantern at the door with snowflakes spinning round it and the way the elm leaves flap against it like yellow butterflies – it's like some place in a fairy tale. And here inside it's as bright and warm as inside a Halloween pumpkin. Those lamps everywhere, and the bottles burning in the mirror. And whenever the door opens, a breath of snow blows in and the lights all shift under and over the shadows. Even if *Casablanca* wasn't on the TV I'd have come tonight.

What'll you have, honey, another one of those? What is that, red wine? Jimmy, another one of those red wines and

I'll have a Jack Daniels. Yes, rocks. And wipe that silly grin off your face, have you no soul, what kind of a man laughs at *Casablanca*? Thanks, Jimmy. Keep it.

Look through that archway, the couples at their little tables, all so solemn and proper with their vintage wine and their candles – look, their heads are hollow, like the candles burnt their eyes out. They might all have stories just as sad as *Casablanca*, but who cares? It's *Casablanca* breaks our hearts, over and over. You cried at the end, I saw you. So did that nice man of yours. Oh, a bar's the place to watch it, a bar's the perfect place. I cry every single time, I can't help myself, it's so noble and sad and innocent and – hell, you know. I couldn't watch it home, anyway. Bill, he's my husband, gets mad when I cry. He walks out. 'Why, am I supposed to stay and watch you slobber over this shit?' he said last time it was on. 'Most people got all they need to slobber about in real life.'

'You're what *I* got,' I said right back.

That's him there, over at the pool table. That your man he's talking to? I thought so. They're lighting up cigarettes and getting acquainted. Isn't that a coincidence? He looks a nice easy-going kind of a guy. But then so does Bill. I love Bill, I love him a lot. I've known that man thirteen years, I could tell you things . . . I'm not blind to anything about Bill, I love him anyway. He loves *me*, though it doesn't feel like being loved much of the time. He needs me. He has to punish me for that. There he is, an older man than he acts. His hair has a grey sheen and his skin hangs loose all over, see the crazed skin on his neck. He's affable and a bit loud with the drink, everybody's pal. Well, when we get home there won't be a word out of him. Under the skin and the smile he's a bitter, fearful man and nobody gets close to him.

He's a second comer, for one thing. He can't forget that. He's my second husband. Yours is a second comer too, is he, honey? Don't mind me sticking my nose in. It's just I can tell. You two are a mite too considerate, too careful with one another, know what I mean? It shows, that's all, if you can read the signs. So what if you are Australians. Oh no. Look, I don't mean you haven't got a nice relationship. But it's only the first time you give your whole self. After that, like it or not, you hold back. You've gotten wise – and you can't pretend *other*wise!

We've been married ten years this Thursday – Thanksgiving Day. You got to laugh. Cheers. Isn't that something, though. My first marriage never got to double figures. I had twenty years alone in between.

Do you remember the first time you saw *Casablanca*? Mine was in 1943, when it first came out, on my honeymoon with Andy. That's reason enough to cry. Bill knows. It's something he can't stand to be reminded of. He pretends it's only Rick and Ilsa making me *slobber*. Men – you tell a man the truth about your life, you end up paying for *ever*. Remember that.

1943! Andy was nineteen, I was seventeen, his ship was sailing for Europe in a week. Our parents said no, you're too young, but we said we'd only run away, so they gave in. We had one weekend for a honeymoon in New York City. The hotel was an awful old ruin – it still is – full of cockroaches and noisy plumbing. We were so embarrassed, you could hear every drop, every trickle. Our room was on the top floor. Through the fire escape we could see the river, and the moon in the mist like a brass knob behind a curtain, and the lights of Manhattan. So it's not a bed of roses, Andy said: it's a bed of lights instead. We saw *Casablanca* and we cried. We were such babies. He was going to be a hero and I was going to wait . . . We danced round the room like Rick and Ilsa did. We sure didn't sleep much. We didn't even know how to *do* it, you know. We were scared. Oh, we soon got the hang of it. And then his ship sailed.

He came back, oh, he came back. He'd won medals in Italy, he was a hero. But he wouldn't ever talk about it. Whatever happened over there, it finished Andy. He started drinking, then he lost his job, and soon he couldn't hold down any job, he just drank and gambled and played the black market. He'd come home once, twice a week, then sleep for days . . .

One night he started hitting me. Everything was my fault, he said. Then he cried. He promised he never would again. I was fool enough to believe it. If they've hit you once and gotten away with it, honey, you're in trouble. It can only get worse.

So, one night I woke up on the kitchen floor. The table lamp was still on, the beer that he spilt looked like butter melting under it. I remember I saw the pattern of brown triangles on the linoleum every time my eyes came open, they looked wet and red, but I couldn't see sharp enough to be sure. The window was black – so it was still night time – and had silver edges like knives where he smashed it. The curtain was half torn down, sopping up the beer on the table and moving in the wind, a white curtain like a wedding veil. *Help me*! I called out. My head felt crushed. The wind must have blown my hair on my face, hair was stuck to it. A long way away something was – snuffling. My nose was flat on my cheek, red bubbles blew out. Andy *wasn't there*. I held my head still and pulled myself up by the table leg: broken glasses, slabs of the window pane, the wet curtain, but no note. No nothing. The room was going all watery and dim as if the floor was hot as fire and yet it was so icy when I lay down, I pulled the curtain down over me to keep warm.

It wasn't till morning that I saw he'd taken all his stuff. God knows there wasn't much, poor Andy. Then I got started all over again: *Don't leave me! Don't leave me alone now! I love you!* Even now I dream – I wake up and for a moment I'm on that floor again knowing I've lost Andy, he's gone for *ever*. Oh, I've never gotten over it.

I'm sorry. Don't be embarrassed. I'll be all right in a moment. Thank you, yes, another Jack Daniels would be nice. Yes, thank you.

Funny thing was, when I got up off the floor next day and my nose was smashed and my eyes looked like two squashed plums and I was shaking so hard I thought my teeth would crack – I ran out into the street in case I could see him and maybe catch him up and all the time I was whimpering, *After all you've done to me, you just get up and go?* I looked in the kitchen window. It was empty, all shadowy gold behind the edges of glass.

Another funny thing – I had a vision in the night, a ballerina came in. (I wanted to be a dancer, I was good, but first the War started, then I got married . . .) Anyway, this ballerina in white was waving her arms and bowing. It must have been the curtain that I saw. She bent down to lift me then she lay beside me, sobbing, I remember that.

Look at us there in the mirror, like two ghosts among the whisky bottles. Okay, Jimmy, laugh. He thinks I'm admiring myself. I'm not that far gone, though I'm getting there. Cheers. Is that really me, that scrawny thing with the spiky grey hair? You'd never think I was a ballet dancer. Bill hates ballet. He says that because the pain and exertion and ugliness aren't allowed to show, it's one big lie. Tinsel and sweat, he says. Dancers smell like horses, someone famous says, so Bill has to read it to me out of the newspaper. Horses aren't any less beautiful for the way they smell, I say. Horses are dancers too and dancers love them. Anyway, I say, I like the way they smell. You would, he says, you're not what you'd call fussy, are you. Now wasn't that asking for it? *No, well, I married you!* I let it pass, though, and he gives me points for not saying it: just a flicker of the eyelids, but enough.

Most of our quarrels end like that. They're harmless. Nothing Bill says or does can get to the quick of me like it did with Andy whether he meant it or not. Bill can make me ache with misery when he wants, but somewhere deep down inside me now there's this little tough muscle braces itself so the barbs can't go too far in. Bill knows. He's the same. Maybe by now it would have been like that with

Andy, who knows? I don't even know if he's alive or dead. My parents came and made me get a divorce. They told him I said he couldn't see me or the kids ever again.

Let me tell you the *worst* thing – let's have another drink? – the worst thing – oh, God, I've never told a living soul this. Jimmy, more of these and have one on me, okay? The worst thing is, when he had me on the floor that night – just pushed me down – and started smashing things and yelling that he wanted *out*, I rolled over and hung on to his trouser leg for dear life and begged him not to leave me. I just wouldn't let go. I – slobbered, and howled and – and I kissed his muddy shoe. So he slammed his other shoe in my face. That's when my nose got broken. I mean, that's why.

I thank God the kids weren't home, they didn't see that. They saw him hit me other times, but not that. They were only little. Rick was about five, Ilsa was just a baby. Something like that, though – if they saw it happen, it'd leave a scar on them. 'I won't let Daddy hurt you,' Ricky used to say to me. They were at my parents' place in New Jersey because I had to get a job so I couldn't look after them. We called them Rick and Ilsa – well, *you* know why! Ilsa's married, she's in Alaska now, she's a nurse. Rick's dead. He got killed in Vietnam. Got a medal doing it, too. If his Daddy ever heard about it, I suppose he must have felt proud. Or maybe not.

Don't get me wrong, I believe in sacrifice, and love and honour and loyalty, even if it turns out they were wasted – else why would I love *Casablanca*? Rick and Ilsa, they had something or someone they'd give up everything for. I only wish I still did. Real people have their moments of glory. Time goes on for them though, they can't live up to it. But the glory lives on in memory. Bill won't see that. Face facts, he says. You and your glory and your wallowing in the past. It's shit, that's all it is, shit preserved in syrup. That's better than shit preserved in vinegar, the way yours is, I say. Oh, that's good, he says. Make with the witty repartee, babe, you know I dig that. (Bill can never let go of anything. All his past is still there inside of him, pickled.) Why better, honey? Shit's still shit, he says then. Who knows the truth? I say. You refuse to, *he* says, and round and round we go.

What you never really get over, I suppose, is finding out love's not enough. Loving someone's no *use*. And you only find out the hard way. No one can tell you. You believe in love when you're young, you believe it's for-ever, it's the only thing that matters, it'll save you both, if you just hang in there and give more and more. I wonder if Ilsa would have gone with Rick – given up everything and gone with him – would it have ended up with her on the floor with her nose smashed? You never know.

Here they come. Look, they're wondering what we're saying. Look at those suspicious eyes and butter-wouldn't-melt smiles of theirs! Your man's been watching you all this time. Here's looking at you, kid! Easy to see you're new. It's great while it lasts, make the most. The couples have had their wine and candlelight and now they're leav-ing. Don't you just love a black and white night like this after snow, when it echoes? And you slide and fall down on top of each other all the way and rub each other's feet dry and warm once you're inside. Okay, fellers, home time? I've lost my coat. Thanks, honey. I feel so lit up it's a wonder you can't see me shining through it! I'm sure I don't know why I've been telling you the story of my life. You cried at the end of *Casablanca*. I suppose that's why.

'Can I read that?'
'Read what?'
Her hands have instinctively spread across the pages of blue scrawl. He raises his eyebrows: 'What you've been writing half the night.'
She passes them over her shoulder. The couch creaks and the pages rustle until at last he tosses them back on the

table and goes to make coffee. She stares at them, sweat prickling her. The heating is on full.

'Thank you,' she says when he brings her mug.

'Is this finished?'

'Oh, for now, anyway. I was just coming to bed – I'm sorry. Haven't you been asleep?'

'I used to respect writers rather a lot,' he murmurs. 'Now I'm not sure.'

'You're writing your thesis on one.'

'Mmm. There's writing and writing. To my mind this –' he points – 'is more like scavenging.' He waits while she swallows hot coffee. 'Perhaps if you wore a badge, a brand on your forehead that meant: *Beware of the scavenger*? Then people would know they were fair game.'

'You think *that's* being *fair*?'

'She trusted you, it seems, with the story of her life.'

'I hope I can do it justice.'

'Justice.' He sighs.

She has nothing to say. He finishes his coffee sip by sip, takes his mug and rinses it, then comes back to stand behind her chair. Her mug is clenched in both hands; the light of the two lamps blurs in her coffee.

'I am not to figure in anything you write,' comes the smooth voice again. 'Never. I hope you understand that.'

Hardly breathing, she cranes her neck forward to have a sip of coffee, but he grabs the mug from her and slams it down on the table, where it breaks. Coffee spurts up and splashes brown and blue drops over her pages. This time she knows better than to move until his footsteps creak away across the boards. His chair scrapes. She hears a match strike in the room beyond, and a sigh as he breathes smoke in.

WHITE FRIDAY

IN A ROOM somewhere Barbara wakes in anguish and lies with her eyes shut, having dreamt someone has died. Who? All that is left is the muddy trampled grass at a graveside, one mourner with her hair dark with rain over her face. Bells in towers clang. She opens blank eyes on a strange white room where she makes a void, a vortex. Still, the bells: more than most other mornings. This is Friday. And this is Greece, yes, Hydra: this is the hotel. She creeps over baked floor-tiles to push the shutters open on nothing but sunlight. '*Seismos einai?*' someone outside shouts. '*Pyrkaia!*' comes the answer. Not an earthquake. A house is on fire.

Tall smoke from a white house high on the hilltop lays itself flat over the town and the harbour. The sea clouds over. Bells in the square clock tower toll, bells in the filigree one, bells further away; then the clock strikes the half-hour. Seven-thirty. '*Kai nero den echei!*' And there is no water! Even if there were, there is no road up to there, only cobbled stairways, and only donkeys to carry it. Shouts echo in the streets. Figures are massing under the stout white walls. Sprouting at the eaves, flames hang like corncobs stored for winter. They are no brighter than corn in the smoky sunlight. Then with a turbulence in the smoke and a great shout the roof caves in.

Late autumn, on a dry island. Yesterday she walked along the cliff road, past the headland with the cannons and the windmill, hoping it led to the monastery that hung among the rocks in a white silence. Here and there an olive, a cypress. But it led to smoke rising, and an avalanche of rotting rubbish poured down to a gulf like a slit in the sky with a rowing boat anchored. The wind ripped tufts of fire out. Furry bodies moved: cats, spitting, cringing, hundreds of them among the charring papers and tooth-edged cans and the bones of roasted animals.

The grave in the dream was not my mother's, she thinks, though it was in Australia. My mother was cremated. Whose, then? Whose hair trickled rain?

Her arms are clinging to the marble window sill as if to ice. She comes inside. With the immersion heater she boils water in her teapot that she takes everywhere – pure white but for two black flecks on the curve under the handle, like moles in an armpit – then adds the tealeaves. She makes her bed the island way, smoothing the starched sheet, folding the blanket at the foot; pours the tea into her mug; sits on the blanket to drink it. The room has warmed, breathing the smoke in. A beautiful room, its ceiling has dark brown ribs that match the shutters and the slatted bench on which she leaves her bag and *Memoirs of Hadrian* open face-down. She reads a few pages aloud every night, her hands warm round the mug, while tea steams in her face and the room hums round her.

The day she came she wrote in her diary:

This is a place of serenity. Wherever I live I want white walls and the sun coming in. Folded all day in warm light, after dark I would turn on all the lamps. When I went out, a lamp left burning would wait.

Now she opens her diary with her free hand and writes:

A solid house on the hill, like this hotel, burned to ashes as I watched – no water to save it.

A drop of tea splashes her white thigh. Wiping the stain away, she remembers the poem she scrawled on an envelope before she slept – yes, there it is – and copies it into the diary.

Winter-white, my thighs
are rippled, high-water-marked:
fine like rice paper.

She canters down stairways bright with fallen leaves between solid houses with pipe-tiled roofs and heavy doors, blue, red, green, that close over courtyards and have as knockers iron heads of lions or goddesses or ringed hands. Iron bars on the windows curve plumply out like grooves in pumpkins. Cats sunning themselves on door-steps cringe as her shadow falls. Flies burn bronze in the donkey dung. At souvenir shops she asks where the O.T.E. is: faces open to her once she speaks in Greek. She has to ring the man she loves in Australia. After these weeks apart, he might prefer her not to. She recoils from the thought that, taken by surprise, he might betray – annoyance? But the dream has alarmed her; and the fire. She has to.

The O.T.E. office is a stale, dingy hall, with an impatient queue for every telephone. When her turn comes she dials again and again: whistles, clicks, silence. At last there are five double rings and then he speaks.

And he is pleased to hear her voice!

He has left the taps running to fill the bath, with his children and their toys in it already, so he can't talk long. Of course, Friday – his children have come down. She tells him she had this dream. Well, he is all right, he says, and so are the children. Everything he talks about makes her heart sink, he is so far away. She says she will be back next Friday. Good, he says. In fact she is in two minds. She has not confirmed her booking; she might stay here. Good-bye, they both say.

The cashier hides a smile. The call has cost her 2850 drachmas, about $30. The bath must have overflowed.

They are all splashing, laughing, in his bathroom in its downy light (it is evening there). A spiderweb strung high on the window frame catches on each movement of the air. Spiderthreads rig a toy yacht with no sails on the shelf. Weeks since she was there. And she might stay here.

Or stay in Athens, where the olives hung ripe two weeks ago, oozing oil, among the ruins and the statues. Or in Thessaloniki, where three weeks ago the yellow leaves froze stiff, and pomegranates blazed, where her sons and their father live now. Darker, heavier boys than she remembers, they sat in waterfront squares at sunset, eating *loukoumades* with her, hotly exchanging glances and giggles with each other. Syrupy kisses they pressed on her lips; goodbye, Mum. She came to Greece to see them.

Only this minute, sun-blinded at the door of the O.T.E., does she think her dream might have meant *them*.

Surely the grave was in Australian? Still, she turns and queues again: rings Thessaloniki. Their father is curt. Everyone is all right. The boys are out. At school, yes. No, never mind. Yes. Goodbye.

Past saddled donkeys and boats she walks along the road round the point into a warm wind, hoping to find the sea cave. Soon she comes to platforms, cannons, broken concrete steps. Dribbling rust, the iron ladders in the rocks have their feet in the ruffled sea. She climbs down one to dip her hands and face for the first time in years in the Aegean – warm, salty, fine to swim in, though the sun has clouded over. Further round she finds the cave, a dome of dark blue light with a hole in the top, a hollow whale of a cave. She would love to swim into it, if people, donkeys, even gravel trucks, would stop going past. Suddenly a dozen Japanese tourists with cameras are clambering on the rocks. Wishing she could turn transparent in the water – surely there are fish that do? – she goes and sits out of sight beside a small blowhole breathing like a dolphin. Across the water are cloud-pale hills in folds; threads of smoke blow off them. Close to shore a fishing boat throbs past, its seabirds squealing in loops. The sun is more like a full moon, shifting among screens of the mist.

Another parade of tourists is coming near.

Panting, she scrambles uphill. A scatter of sweet rain furs the sea behind her, pricks her skin. Birds cry out in astonishment. The darkening earth breathes out warm smells. Above the white windmill on the far side of the harbour a rainbow comes into being. Out of the rusty grey rocks where she is, pine trees and gums are growing, Australian gums, and thorns and thistles. Her feet slither on red pine needles. She sits on a stone wall to get her breath. Hens stalk away. A rooster raises its throat, dripping scarlet, to drink rain. A ladybird like a small tortoise will not move from her sleeve.

Stones rattling from above her make her jump. Startled, a white goat skips off smiling, her rope like a tufted tail behind her. 'Bebekaaa!' screeches a hag in a low doorway. The goat nibbles, bridles, falters towards Barbara; then lets her pick up the tuft and lead her home.

The hag fondles the long white ears. 'Thank you, my girl.'

The town clock strikes twelve and suddenly all the bells are ringing again. Barbara stares. 'God protect us': the hag crosses herself.

New smoke has risen over the hill, from the burnt house. They can see it from here, roofless, crammed to its white lintels with ashes. Rubble has spilt out wherever doors and windows were. A smell of wet ashes comes on the wind. But soon the smoke frills away.

'Whose house was it?' asks Barbara in Greek.

'A rich man's. They live in Athens. Don't tell me you're Greek?'

'I was.'

'How come?'

'My sons are. And their father. I'm Australian, though.'

'Australians sometimes live here. You I've never seen before.'

'We mostly lived in Thessaloniki. I've just been there to see the boys.' And angrily: 'They were born in Australia, though.' This is a lie. She is surprised at herself.

'How many? Who looks after them?'

'Two. His new wife. She's pregnant. His mother helps her. The older boy started high school in September.'

The goat tugs, the tuft of the rope jerks free; flicking her tail, she stops high on the slope to gaze down benignly. With a sigh the woman turns her back. 'Your Greek is good,' she says. 'Why not live here?' She screws up cunning eyes.

'I can't decide.' Barbara smiles. 'We still write letters. Ring, on special occasions. But we're not –'

'Over there (Bebeka!) you have someone.'

'Not since my mother died.'

In her hand she adds to a letter she has been writing to him, not to be posted because won't she get back first?

I'm using up my mother's shampoos; frugality was dinned into me as a little girl. Guiltily I threw away her butts of lipsticks – the show of bravery they made.

Who, I wonder, will use up what I leave behind?

Letters never sent, or sent but not answered; if answered, not answered to the point but at an angle to it: this is how it has been with him all along, in spite of what they wanted. She suspects that it will be in silence that they lose each other, by which time he won't care.

After the silence of respect for death: 'Condolences, my girl. You have a man, I meant.'

'Oh. Well, I don't have – not *have*. There is a man I –'

'But not in wedlock.' Her face closes.

'Ah. No.'

And the woman is shrugging disparagingly: 'Your own children are here?' And turning: 'Ach! Now look where she's got to. Bebeka!' Like a baby's her grin shows gums and two stumps of bottom teeth. In a terraced tomato patch the goat props, stutters. The woman is clambering up. 'Beh–beh–ka! Come back!'

'Goodbye.' Barbara calls.

'Yes. God go with you.'

Bebeka means baby girl. Barbara is sorry not to have

had a girl. (*He* has one.) In a sense it's not too late; and yet it is. She has been alone too long. The membranes that bind her to other lives have worn too thin to sustain her in motherhood. *Over there, you have someone*. Her only living relatives are the boys. Their names and the Thessaloniki address are in her passport: *in case of death or accident*. One day they will stand holding a letter from the Embassy.

Bebeka, dislodging a rock too many, smashing through the crust of tiles on some ruined house, is sure to break her neck.

Barbara sees the old woman turn to stare back over her shoulder, her hands knotted on a root in the hill.

The drizzle has stopped. I weigh lightly on the earth, Barbara thinks, picking her way round and down: what does it matter if I live here, or there? If I sold my mother's house I could afford to live here. Her abrupt and resentful spirit stalks me through its narrow rooms and shares her old bed with me. Under the dust her mirrors in the morning startle me with a face not yet hers. I will sell it. If I want to I can even go from island to island.

A cobweb quivers on his evening window.

Under dark arches and along stairways flashing with puddles she makes her way down to the harbour.

A cruise ship has docked and all the shops are open waiting. At the corner *taverna* near the monastery most of the outside tables are taken already. On the steps down to it she almost treads on white fur lying there – a sprawled cat. She recoils, crouching in horror. It has shat itself, its twitching haunch is pasted with shit and blowflies. Froth drips from its jaw. Aware of her presence, it rasps itself round on the whitewash, its paws stretched out to her. Its eye is fixed and its dry tongue points. Passersby stare, but at her. She walks away.

The thought of eating makes her sick, but she finds a table against the sunny wall and asks for a bottle of *retsina*, since they only have bottles. Everywhere the cats are lying in wait, under the tables or on rush-bottomed chairs in the sun; some snuffle and retch, some vibrate with greed, some doze, paws folded. After two glasses of the woody wine she wanders inside and orders stuffed tomatoes. Thick bread comes with it: she eats it all, mopping up the red oil with the last crust. On the whitewashed wall at her back is a yellow light in the shape of a bottle of *retsina*.

A black cat stretches out a paw, then it is in a blond woman's lap, its tail a flagpole. 'Oh, what a lovely boy': she strokes its cheeks. A laughing group of Japanese tourists passing by takes everyone's photo. A team of donkeys clatters past. 'The Japanese! The new rich,' blares an Englishwoman. Cooing, the blonde flicks haricot beans one by one under the table – no, not beans: the fried eyes of fish. A scuffle of cats erupts.

A boy who looks like Barbara's sons charges the cats with a straw broom. 'Oh, don't!' Barbara calls in Greek. His impudent eyes meet hers. With a yell he scoops a tabby up, thumps it against the wall. The blonde screams. Resentfully the cook grabs the boy's shoulders and marches him inside. More donkeys plod nodding past.

Half a bottle of *retsina* throws its shape on the hot wall. When it is gone, Barbara stumbles away. The white cat is motionless now in the shade. She finds the stairway to the hotel, her head swarming, and collapses on her starched sheet.

The bells for vespers half-wake her, and the rush of rain. When she wakes properly, shivering and dry-mouthed, the sun has just set and a cruise ship on its way out is making the dim red harbour water roll. Yellow lights come flickering on. *Souroupo*, she says aloud, thinking what a lovely word for twilight: and *plio* for a boat, that sound of parted water. *To plio fevgei souroupo*. Where is it going? Even so high up she can hear and smell the sea.

As she is picking up her teapot, it slips out of her hands to smash into the basin. Shocked, she turns on the basin light and stoops in her shadow picking up the glossy fragments and the wet tealeaves. You stupid, she tells the mirror: look at you mourning for it. As if it were alive. She washes her hands that smell like wet ashes.

Now that a light is on she closes the shutters; rainy air still flows in. Before the real rain starts again, she pulls on her yellow slicker and splashes down stairways to the bright shops, open again, to buy her evening yoghurt in the grocery she likes, a tunnel of stiff salt cod, opened tubs and barrels, chandeliers of sausage. Already rain is prickling the puddles. The red light at the headland is spilt wide. The cobbles of the harbour front, always so glossy at night that they look wet, are streaming, glimmering now. Rain falls from boats into yellow water.

At a turn in the stairway a man mutters urgently to a woman whose long hair hides her; hearing footsteps, she winces, lifts a face aflash with light, rain – tears? A *taverna* further along has its music bottled up in golden glass, and its sedate families in rows. Three girls passing her arm-in-arm chant in chords, '*Ka-li ny-chta.*' Inside the Frondistirion Anglikis Glossis an Englishwoman articulates: 'He has five pounds in his wallet. She has five pounds . . .' A dog howls.

She gets back just before the heavy rain breaks. In the still light of her room she parts the shutters to look out at all the lighted windows (one blank and black where the burnt walls stand); all the yellow cascading under streetlamps. The usual shouts and laughs from the evening streets are muffled, voices underwater. A church bell chimes.

A rich man's. They live in Athens.

The shutters closed, she sits cross-legged on the sheet to eat the yoghurt, blandly sour with a crinkled skin, and spoonfuls of honey she curls out of her honey-jar. She licks her syrupy lips. Still loud, the rain; a voice in a bubble reads shadowy pages of *Memoirs of Hadrian*. Is it raining in Athens, on the statues and the olives? Raining in Thessaloniki? The boys live there. Raining where he is?

Naked in her white bed she imagines herself in his. She strokes his arms and shoulders, strokes him all over and kisses his shaggy head as it bends to her nipple. He has long eyelashes like shadows. The dark hairs of his body press soft against her. When he falls asleep he lies breathing in her arms, as confiding as a child (as his children). But he is lent, not given. He has said – to her, to others – that he can never imagine living with her. He asked once, 'If you had a man, would you want to have another child?' The words spread silently inside her like blood pooling. How should she have answered? What does it mean anyway – *have*?

Why did he ask?

Lying flat, she remembers the death that the old man flicking worry beads told her about on her first day here, in the grocery she likes. A girl, having grown up on this island, in Australia dressed herself again in all her white wedding clothes and put her head in her gas oven. Why? No one knew why.

This has been a white day of bad dreams and omens.

Nevertheless, regardless, she leans over and on the Monday page of her diary she writes in large capitals:

O.T.E.: RING AND CONFIRM RETURN FLIGHT THURS. 3.45 A.M.

She slips it under the pillow. She is going back, it seems. Why? Is this how decisions should be made or make themselves? Never mind. This is as good a way as any.

In Australia Saturday morning has begun. He and his children are waking up in his white front room where trees make the sunlight flutter on them. A world away, in a few hours chimes and church bells will wake her: bells flung on ropes from edge to edge, great voices bursting through the shutters, slashes of the sun.

A MAN IN THE LAUNDRETTE

SHE NEVER wants to disturb him but she has to sometimes, as this room in which he studies and writes and reads is the only way in and out of his apartment. Now that he has got up to make coffee in the kitchen, though, she can put on her boots and coat and rummage in the wardrobe for the glossy black garbage bag where they keep their dirty clothes, and not be disturbing him. 'I'll only be an hour or two,' she says quickly when he comes back in. She holds up the bag to show why.

'Are you sure?' His eyebrows lift. 'It must be my turn by now.' They were scrupulous about such matters when she first moved in.

'I'm sure. I must get out more. Meet the people.' She shrugs at his stare. 'I want to see what I can of life in the States, after all.'

'Not to be with me.'

She smiles. 'Of course to be with you. You know that.'

'I thought you had a story you wanted to finish.'

'I had. It's finished. You know you don't have time to go, and I like going.'

He stands there unsmiling, holding the two mugs. 'I made you a coffee,' he says.

'Thanks.' She perches on the bed and drinks little scalding sips while, turned in his chair, he stares out at the sky.

His window is above the street and on brighter afternoons than this it catches the whole heavy sun as it goes down. He always works in front of the window but facing the wall, a dark profile.

He says, 'Look how dark it's getting.'

'It's just clouds,' she says. 'It's only a little after three.'

'Still. Why today? Saturday.'

'Why not? That's your last shirt.'

'It's mostly my clothes, I suppose.' It always is. She washes hers in the bathroom basin and hangs them on the pipes. He has never said that this bothers him; but then she has never asked. He shrugs. 'You don't know your way round too well. That's all.'

'I do! Enough for the laundrette.'

'Well. Okay. You've got Fred's number?'

She nods. Fred, who lives on the floor above, has the only telephone in the building and is sick of having to fetch his neighbours to take calls. She rang Fred's number once. She gets up without finishing her coffee.

'Okay. Take care.' He settles at the table with his back turned to her and to the door and to his bed in which she sleeps at night even now, lying with the arm that shades her eyes chilled and stiff, sallowed by the lamp, while he works late. Sighing, he switches this lamp on now and holds his coffee up to it in both hands, watching the steam fray.

Quietly she shuts the door.

The apartment houses have lamps on already under their green awnings. They are old three-storey brick mansions, red ivy shawling them. Old elms all the way along his street are golden-leaved and full of quick squirrels: the air is bright with leaves falling. The few clumps that were left this morning of the first snow of the season have all dripped away now. As she comes down the stoop a cold wind throws leaves over her, drops of rain as sharp as snow prickle her face. The wind shuffles her and her clumsy bag around the corner, under the viaduct, down block after weedy block of the patched bare roadway. The laundrette seems further away than it should be. Has she lost her way? No, there it is at last on the next corner: D.K.'s Bar and Laundrette. With a shudder, slamming the glass door behind her, she seals herself in the warm steam and rumble, and looks round.

There are more people here than ever before. Saturday would be a busy day, she should have known that. Everywhere solemn grey-haired black couples are sitting in silence side by side, their hands folded. Four small black girls with pigtails and ribbons erect on their furrowed scalps give her gap-toothed smiles. A scowling fat white woman is the only other white. All the washers are going. Worse, the coins in her pocket turn out not to be quarters but Australian coins, useless. All she has in U.S. currency is a couple of dollar notes. There is a hatch for change with a buzzer in one wall, opening, she remembers, into a back room of the bar; but no one answers it when she presses the buzzer. Too shy to ask anyone there for the change, she hurries out to ask in D.K.'s Bar instead. In the dark room into which she falters, wind-whipped, her own head meets her afloat among lamps in mirrors. Eyes in smoky booths turn and stare. She waits, fingering her dollar notes, but no one goes behind the bar. She creeps out again. The wind shoves her into the laundrette.

This time she keeps on pressing and pressing the buzzer until a voice bawls, 'Aw, *shit*,' and the hatch thuds open on the usual surly old Irishman in his grey hat.

'Hul*lo*!' Her voice sounds too bright. 'I thought you weren't *here*!' She hands him her two dollars.

'Always here.' He flicks his cigarette. 'Big fight's on cable.' A roar from the TV set and he jerks away, slapping down her eight quarters, slamming the hatch.

She is in luck. A washer has just been emptied and no one else is claiming it. Redfaced, she tips her clothes in. Once she has got the washer churning she sits on a chair nearby with her garbage bag, fumbling in it for her writing pad and pen. She always writes in the laundrette.

She never wants to disturb him, she scrawls on a new page, *but she has to sometimes, as this room in which he studies and writes and reads is the only way in and out of his apartment.*

A side door opens for a moment on to the layered smoke of the bar. A young black man, hefty in a padded jacket, lurches out almost on top of her and stands swaying. His stained white jeans come closer each time to her bent head. She edges away.

Now that he has got up to make coffee in the kitchen, though, she can put on her boots and coat and rummage in the wardrobe for the glossy black garbage bag where they keep their dirty clothes, and not be disturbing him.

'Pretty handwriting,' purrs a voice in her ear. When she stares up, he smiles. Under his moustache he has front teeth missing, and one eyetooth is a furred brown stump. 'What's *that* say?' A pale fingernail taps her pad.

'Uh, nothing.'

'*Show* me.' He flaps the pad over. Its cover is a photograph of the white-hooded Opera House. 'Sydney, Australia,' he spells out. 'You from Australia?'

'Yes.'

'Stayin' long?'

'Just visiting.'

'I *said* are you stayin' *long*?'

'No.'

'Don' like the U-nited States.'

She shrugs. 'It's time I went home.'

'Home to Australia. Well now. My teacher were from Australia, my music teacher. She were a nice Australian lady. She got me into the Yale School of Music.' He waits.

'That's good.' She gives him a brief smile, hunching over her writing pad.

'I'll only be an hour or two,' she says quickly when he comes back in. She holds up the bag to show why.

'Are you sure?' His eyebrows lift. 'It must be my turn by now.'

'What you writin'?'

'A story.'

'Story, huh? I write songs. I'm a musician. I was four years at the Yale School of Music. That's *good*, is it?' He thrusts his face close to hers and she smells rotting teeth and fumes of something – bourbon, perhaps, or rum. So that's what it is: he is drunk. He has a bunched brown paper bag with a bottle in it, which he unscrews with difficulty and wags at her. 'Have some.' She shakes her head. Shrugging, he throws his head back to swallow, chokes and splutters on the floor. He wipes his lips on the back of his hand, glaring round. Everyone is carefully not looking. One small black girl snorts and they all fall into giggles. He bows to them.

'I work in a piana bar, hey *you*, I ain' talkin' to myself.' She looks up. 'That's *bet*ter. My mother and father own it so you wanna hear me sing I get you in for free. Hey, you wanna hear me sing or don't you?' She nods. 'All *right*.' What he sings in a slow, hoarse tremolo sounds like a spiritual, though the few words she picks up make no sense. The black girls writhe. The couples sitting in front of the dryers exchange an unwilling smile and shake of the head.

'You like that, huh?' She nods. 'She *like* that. Now I sing you all another little number I wrote, I write all my own numbers and I call this little number Calypso Blues.' Then he sings more, as far as she can tell, of the same song.

They were scrupulous about such matters when she first moved in.

'I'm sure. I must get out more. Meet the people.' She shrugs at his stare. *'I want to see what I can of life in the States, after all.'*

'Like that one? My mother and father – *hey* – they real rich peoples, ain' just the piana bar, they got three houses. Trucks. Boats too. I don' go along with that shit. Ownin' things, makin' money, that's all shit. What you say your name was? Hey, *you*. You hear me talkin' to you?'

'Uh, Anne,' she lies, her head bowed.

'Pretty.' He leans over to finger her hair. 'Long yeller hair. Real . . . pretty.'

'Don't.'

' "I want to see what I can of life in the States after" –
after *what*?'

'*All*.' She crams the pad into her garbage bag.

'You sha' or somethin'?'

'What?'

'You sha'? You deaf or somethin'? You *shacked*?'

'Oh! Shacked? Shacked – yes, I am. Yes.' She keeps
glancing at the door. The first few times that it was her
turn to do the laundry he came along anyway after a while,
smiling self-consciously, whispering, 'I missed you.' But
not today, she knows. She stares at somebody's clothes
flapping and soaring in a dryer. She could take hers home
wet, though they would be heavy: but then this man
might follow her home.

'So where you live?'

'Never mind,' she mutters.

'What's that?'

'I don't *know*. Oh, down the road.'

'Well, you can tell me.'

'No, I'd – I don't *know* its name.'

'I just wanna talk to you – *Anne*. I just wanna be friends.
You don' wanna be friends, that what you sayin'? You
think I got somethin' nasty in my mind, well I think *you*
do.' He snorts. 'My lady she a white lady like you an' let
me tell *you* you ain' nothin' alongside of her. *You* ain'
nothin'.'

She stares down. He prods her arm. 'Don't,' she says.

'Don' what?'

'Just don't.'

'Hear me, bitch?'

'Don't talk to me like that.'

'Oh, don' talk to you like that? I wanna talk to you, I talk
to you how I like, don't you order *me* roun' tell me how I
can talk to you.' He jabs his fist at her shoulder then holds it
against her ear. 'Go on, look out the door. Expectin'
somebody?'

'My friend's coming.'

'Huh. She expectin' her *friend*.' The couples look back gravely. 'My brothers they all gangsters,' he shouts, 'an' one word from me gets anybody I *want* killed. We gonna kill them *all*.' He is sweaty and shaking now. 'We gonna kill them and dig them up and kill them all *over* again. Trouble with you, Miss Australia, you don' like the black peoples, that's trouble with you. Well we gonna kill you *all*.' He drinks and gasps, licking his lips.

The door opens. She jumps up. With a whoop the wind pushes in two Puerto Rican couples with garbage bags. Leaves and papers come rattling over the floor to her feet. One of the Puerto Ricans buzzes and knocks at the hatch for change, but no one opens it; in the end they pool what quarters they find in their pockets, start their washers and sit in a quiet row on a table. Her machine has stopped now. There is a dryer free. She throws the tangled clothes in, twists two quarters in the slot and sits hunched on another chair to wait.

He has lost her. He spits into the corner, staggering, wiping his sweat with a sleeve, then begs a cigarette from the sullen white woman, who turns scornfully away without a word. 'Bitch,' he growls: a jet of spit just misses her boot. One of the Puerto Ricans offers him an open pack. Mumbling, he picks one, gets it lit, splutters it out and squats shakily to pick it up out of his splash of spit. He sucks smoke in, sighs it out. Staring round, he finds her again and stumbles over. 'Where you get to?' He coughs smoke in her face. His bottle is empty: not a drop comes out when he tips it up over his mouth. 'God*dam*,' he wails, and lets it drop on the floor, where it smashes. 'Goddam mothers, you all givin' me *shit*!'

'No one doin' that,' mutters a wrinkled black man.

He has swaggered up close, his fly almost touching her forehead. '*Don't*,' she says despairingly.

'Don't, don't. Why not? I like you, Miss Australia.' He gives a wide grin. 'Gotta go next door for a minute. Wanna come? No? Okay. Don' nobody bother her now.

Don't nobody interfere. She *my* lady.'

He stumbles to the side door and opens it on a darkness slashed with red mirrors. Once the door shuts the black couples slump and sigh. One old woman hustles the little black girls out on to the street. An old man leans forward and says, 'He your friend, miss?'

'No! I've never seen him before.'

The old man and his wife roll their eyes, their faces netting with anxious wrinkles. 'You better watch out,' he says.

'What if he follows me home?'

They nod. 'He a load of trouble, that boy. Oh, his poor mother.'

'Maybe he'll stay in there and won't come back?' she says.

'Best thing is you call a cab, go on home. They got a pay phone here.'

'Oh, *where?*'

'In the bar.'

'*Where!*'

The side door slams open, then shut, and they all sit back guiltily. She huddles, not looking round. Her clothes float down in the dryer, so she opens it and stoops into the hot dark barrel to pick them out, tangled still and clinging to each other. Suddenly he is bending over her, his hands braced on the wall above the dryer, his belly thrust hard against her back. She twists angrily out from under him, clutching hot shirts.

'Now stop that! That's enough!'

'Not for me it ain', not yet.'

'Leave me alone!'

'I wanna talk. Wanna talk to you.'

'No! Go away!' She crams the clothes into her garbage bag.

'Hey, you not well, man,' mumbles the old black. 'Better go on home now. Go on home.'

'Who you, man, you gonna tell *me* what to do?' He

throws a wide punch and falls to the floor. With a shriek of rage and terror the old woman runs to the side door and pounds on it. It slaps open, just missing her, and two white men tumble in.

'Okay,' one grunts. 'What's trouble here?'

'Where you *been*? You supposed to keep *order*!' she wails, and the old man hushes her. The young man is on his knees, shaking his frizzy head with both his hands.

With gestures of horrified embarrassment to everyone she sees watching her, she swings the glass door open on to the dim street. A man has followed her: one of the two Puerto Ricans. 'Is okay. I see you safe home,' he says, and slings her bag over his shoulder.

'Oh, thank you! But your wife's still in there.'

'My brother is there.' He takes her arm, almost dragging her away.

'He was so drunk,' she says. 'What made him act like that. I mean, why me?'

His fine black hair flaps in the wind. 'You didn't handle him right,' he says.

'What's *right*?'

'You dunno. Everybody see that. Just whatever you did, you got the guy mad, you know?'

They are far enough away to risk looking back. He is out on the road, his body arched, yelling at three white men: the old Irishman in the hat has joined the other two and they are barring his way at the door of the laundrette. There is something of forebearance, even of compunction, in their stance. 'They'll leave him alone, won't they?' she asks.

He nods. 'Looks like they know him.'

He has seen her all the way to the corner before she can persuade him, thanking him fervently, that she can look after herself from here on. He stands guard in the wind, his white face uneasily smiling whenever she turns to grin and wave him on. The wind thrashes her along their street. In the west the clouds are fraying, letting a glint of light through, but the streetlamps are coming on already with a milky fluttering, bluish-white, among the gold tossings of the elms.

A squirrel on their fence fixes one black resentful eye on her: it whirls and stands erect, its hands folded and its muzzle twitching, until abruptly it darts away, stops once to look back, and the silver spray of its tail follows it up an elm.

The lamp is on in his window – none of the windows in these streets has curtains – and he is still in front of it, a shadow. She fumbles with her key. Rushing in, she disturbs him.

'Am I late? Sorry! There was this terrible man in the laundrette.' Panting, she leans against the dim wall to tell him the story. Halfway through she sees that his face is stiff and grey.

'You're thinking I brought it on myself.'

'Didn't you?'

'By going out, you mean? By not wanting to be rude?' He stares. 'No, you wouldn't.'

'What did I do that was wrong?'

'A man can always tell if a woman fancies him.'

'Infallibly?' He shrugs. 'I led him on, is that what you mean?'

'Didn't you?'

'Why would I?'

'You can't seem to help it.'

'Why do you think that?'

'I've seen you in action.'

'*When?*'

'Whenever you talk to a man, it's there.'

'This is sick,' she says. He shakes his head. 'Well, *what's* there?' But he turns back without a word to the lamplit papers on his table.

Shivering, she folds his shirts on the wooden settle in the passage, hangs up his trousers, pairs his socks. Her few things she drops into her suitcase, open on the floor of the wardrobe; she has never properly unpacked. Now she never will. There is no light in this passage, at one end of which is his hood of yellow lamplight and at the other the twin yellow bubbles of hers, wastefully left on while she was out. The tall windows behind her lamps are nailed shut. A crack in one glitters like a blade. Wasps dying of the cold have nested in the shaggy corners. In the panes, as in those of his window, only a greyness like still water is left of the day.

But set at eye level in the wall of the passage where she is standing with her garbage bag is a strip of window overgrown with ivy, one small casement of which she creeps up at night from his bed to prise open, and he later to close: and here a slant of sun strikes. Leaves all the colours of fire flicker and tap the glass.

'Look. You'd think it was stained glass, wouldn't you? Look,' she is suddenly saying aloud. 'I'll never forget this window.'

He could be a statue or the shadow of one, a hard edge to the lamplight. He gives no sign of having heard.

Wasps are slithering, whining over her window panes. One comes bumbling in hesitant orbits round her head. It has yellow legs and rasps across her papers jerking its long ringed belly. She slaps it with a newspaper and sweeps it on to the floor, afraid to touch it in case a dead wasp can still sting, if you touch the sting. Then she sits down at the table under the lamps with her writing pad and pen and scrawls on, though her hand, she sees, is shaking.

'Not to be with me.'

She smiles. 'Of course to be with you. You know that.'

'I thought you had a story you wanted to finish.'

'I had. It's finished.'

FIRE AND FLOOD

AT THE best of times I was – am – far from being a man of action. Joan was sometimes irritated by what she called my immovability. I've come to a standstill now.

For the past few months I've been living in an upstairs flat in Melbourne, in a street that runs alongside a railway cutting. My bedroom has two windows: the one high over the bed looks south, the other east on to the street. I leave both blinds up all night. From time to time a car grunts and slides away and its lights fling the sudden shape of the east window in at me. There is a silver birch and a streetlamp beyond it which inks in all over the room the shapes of its spotted branches and its leaves fewer each day. On rainy nights the branches themselves are black. Edged and beaded with lamplight they quiver under their weight of water. At full moon a whiter backwash floods the branches on the wall.

Tree of light and death, heaventree. For the time being I need to live alone inside a web of black branches. My mind shies away. It must take them in.

Standing there at the window I can see the top half of the trains that pass in the cutting. All evening yellow train-loads of people come and go, sitting up straight, some with their hands at the edges of newspapers. (I hardly ever read a newspaper now.) A pulse trembles in my walls whenever a train passes; if I lean against them I can feel it.

Last night a woman woke me, shouting: 'You've given me nothing in four years!' A silence. 'Four years! *Nothing.*'

Wasn't it six? I caught myself thinking: surely it was six?

I gave you all I could, Joan. You must know that. Salvation, absolution – they weren't in my power.

But this was a woman outside, and a man's voice bellowed out once in furious reproach, '*Sarah!*' Only once. And the only answer was the sound of heels tapping away down the street.

I have lost Joan. Lost Sam. The dreams I have of them bare me to the bone.

As one window faces east, if I happen to open my eyes as day breaks (most mornings I do) I see the sky red, and trees still or windflung outspread black against it. I close my eyes and walk on bleeding earth. Lava, the earth's blood, gushes and along its banks, as with a wound, a black scab forms. The hill is smoke and ashes. Flames burst up in a gully of bracken. At their core a boy in bathers is asleep on his back. I scream: 'Sam!' The smile leaves his lips. As I bend forward he breaks up into fire coals like a log on the hearth. The window breathes in on me.

I get up for a glass of water or vodka and sit up in bed sipping it. My hand round the glass absorbs my attention as the sun comes up. The light caught in both flesh and glass fuses them into one red-gold mass. When the sun touches the wall, bird shadows are on the shadows of the branches.

This morning when I went to the other room for a drink, a sparrow had found its way in, I suppose between the blades of the exhaust fan. I heard its chirrup and ruffle of wings. Then the brown egg-shape leaped at the panes. I wound open what windows I could (this room also has two): it battered the fixed ones. Each time it flew through a ray of sunlight it flashed as if on fire. At last it hurtled out into the silver birch and I could wind the windows shut.

On the day of the fires, birds flying high above were overcome by the heat, fell and were burnt. The wings of others caught alight in midair. Falling, they set more bush on fire.

Early that morning Sam and I went to the Cascades to collect samples of water life for him to take to school.

A favourite place of ours, the Cascades were – are – reached by a bush track lit in stripes of green and gold-brown wherever the sun touches the river. Past a quarry the sky opens out over flat rocks and the river is forced down narrow slimy channels, the Cascades. When Sam was small we came to draw with chalks on the grey rocks, and paddle and fish with nets. Soon he graduated to sliding down the channels on plastic garbage bags with the big kids, smack into the deep pool at the bottom. Not this summer, though: the drought had dried up the channels. The river was a chain of dark pools covered with curds of scum like dried vomit.

We found ourselves a hollow out of the hot north wind. Above us the gums tossed and creaked; here ants and skinks tilted their long shadows, and dragonflies sped, then stayed and their wings drilled holes in the air. There were hoppings and writhings at the black lips of the pools. Sam as he dipped his jamjars sent bronze lights swaying. There was a stink of rottenness, too foul to be from the pool: someone had turned a black snake inside out and hung it over a branch, with opal flies for a skin.

The dog chained at the quarry barked. Sam laughed, barking back.

'She's a scorcher today,' people were saying in the streets. 'If a fire gets going today, we've had it.'

'Reckon there'll be a fire, Peter?' Sam said.

Sam called me Peter, not Dad: he was Joan's boy. (I have no children.) He was a few days short of his eighth birthday and after six years together we were father and son all the same.

'There's a cool change on the way,' I said. 'But if a fire does start, you make for the beach with your mother and stay there.'

'They ought to have back-burnt the bush ages ago,' he said. 'That's what Jake reckons.'

Jake was – still is, I suppose – a journalist; his boy Colin was Sam's best mate at school.

'They couldn't have this year because of the drought,' I said. 'Everything's been dry as paper for months now. They couldn't take the risk.'

'He reckons we're in for the big one all right.'

'Big or little, make for the beach and you'll be okay.'

From the school where I taught, in the industrial zone of Moorong, home was a good hour's drive round the coast. It was after four by the time I got halfway – halfway is where you first see the lighthouse on the point – and saw clouds rising over the far cliffs. Storm clouds on the coast come over with the rear and lunge of surf, they have a dark vault and fray out in slow explosions of white. But there was no water in these: they were smoke. Soon after that I nearly went hurtling into a roadblock. They were turning all traffic back and getting ready to evacuate the coastal towns. It's the big one all right, they said. No casualties, as far as they knew.

It was a slow crawl back to Moorong, with a couple of stops at petrol stations to try and ring Joan. From a friend's place in Moorong I kept on dialling our number, then the Beach Hotel (where Joan worked some evenings), until at last I got on to her. The fire had burnt out the fringe of the town, she said: a lot of our friends' houses. It had gone east and wiped out the next two towns. The hills were burning. Our place was safe so far but there'd been spot fires. The cool change was due any minute.

'Sam all right?'

'Yes. He's up at Marie's with Colin. He's gone wild with excitement. Keeps badgering everyone with ideas for fighting the fire. Jake's out on the firetruck.'

'Shouldn't you all stay down near the beach? Look, I'll

drive the long way round, I'll be home in two hours,' I said. 'The inland roads are open, aren't they?'

'No, no, don't,' she said. 'Nobody knows where it's going next. We're all safe where we are so let's stay put. You can come tomorrow.'

So all I know of the day and night of the fires is what Joan and others told me, what I heard at the inquest and read in the papers.

All that morning of intolerable heat Joan worked in her painting shed. After lunch she listlessly did the washing. Before she could peg it all out it dried in one roar of the northerly. Sam came tearing home from school with the news that a bushfire had broken out behind our hills and was heading for the town. As he said it, swollen clouds rolled over the sky. She hurried to unpeg the washing. But it was smoke.

Red and gasping, she and Sam ran to collect books, papers, photographs, her canvases, his toys, the television set, odd pieces of clothing, and cram them into the car. Breathing was painful; between trips they lay on the clammy kitchen linoleum to cool off. Dread and the heat were making her vague. At last she locked up and drove to the foreshore. Standing with Sam at her side in the shallows – a flat sea, milky jade green – she watched the dark rim of the bay burn round to the river mouth. Trees were suddenly crests of flame, then black bones, and fire brimmed in the grass. Horses set free went wandering along the water's edge, mirrored among the clouds.

Schoolmates of Sam's were down at the beach, among them his best mate Colin and his older brother. They swam around together and watched the fires for a while. When they had to go home, Sam begged to be allowed to go with them. They were having good fun. Colin's place was up the hill, but nowhere near the fires: Sam went there most afternoons, didn't he? Colin's mother didn't mind.

Worn down, Joan said he could go.

Some time after sunset – no telling when sunset was, in all the smoke – she walked back and hosed the house down, though it seemed pointless. There was no one in sight. She went in and lay down sweltering in the smoky light of a lamp. Both the radio and the television set were in the boot of the car, down on the foreshore. She rang the hotel: she wasn't feeling up to going to work. But they were short-staffed already, they said, with nearly everyone out at the fires. As they were speaking her lamp went off, and that settled it. The power was off in the house, in the street: in half the town.

So she rang Marie, Colin's mother. The power was on there and the boys were having a great time. She'd keep Sam there until Joan could pick him up after work.

Cars crammed to the roof were still crawling into the main street and the foreshore. Burnt-out families were settling with borrowed bedding in shopfronts and in the school buildings. By now mountains of red-lit smoke hung so low over the river that it seemed that the nearest rooftops were on fire.

As she served the meals in the terrace bar, the flames made their way along the hills, clear in the darkness where in daylight the smoke had hidden them. Yellow gushes of light glowed and sank back. The cool change came: the wind whipped round to the south-west, spitting rain, and took the fire with it.

She had no suspicion until the call came from the hospital, a call she couldn't make sense of. Sick with terror, she ran all the way. Marie was there, and Colin and his brother, moaning in each other's arms. Joan screamed when she saw their hands and their feet, Marie told me later: and again when she saw that Sam wasn't with them.

It seems, piecing stories together, that within minutes of the change their trees and then their eaves, their whole roof, caught fire. As Marie rushed the boys out, still in bathers and thongs but holding around themselves the blankets she had kept soaking in the bath, a burning tree torn up in the squall crashed among them. A thick branch pinned Sam down by the legs; branches all around were blazing. They had to leave him. Marie shoved her boys into the back seat and drove blindly down the hill with the fire all around her. When the engine cut out she steered somehow on to level ground, and firefighters were there to take them on to safety. She told them where Sam was. We'll get him out, they said.

Marie and her boys and Joan were kept at the hospital under sedation. I knew nothing about it. No one knew where to ring me; Joan couldn't remember.

In Moorong we tried station after station on the radio and then the television news: helicopters had got news teams in. According to them, everyone in our town was huddled on the beach or the pier watching the last houses go up. Fires, firestorms, were raging out of control in the hills near Melbourne. There were unconfirmed reports of people being burnt alive, even in cars. (That can't be right, we said. Isn't that what they tell you, stay in your car? But it was right.)

I got on to Joan at the hotel. She was flat out, but calm. She wrote down my friend's number and promised to try to ring after work. I probably won't get through, she said. I knew that.

I rang Marie too. 'We've got off lightly,' she said. Sam was playing cricket in the backyard, so I didn't ask to speak to him.

By then there were a few people at my friend's place, some of them with houses in the fire's path. We went through a fair amount of beer, and after a while we gave up on the radio and the television altogether and even the phone and put on records instead. Someone passed a joint or two around. At some time in the middle of all the confusion and hysteria I stretched out on the hot seagrass matting and went to sleep.

I woke over and over in smoky light – there was ash in the smoke clouds over Moorong – and then alone in darkness, sure that it must be daybreak and time to get going; until at last it was.

I drove home against a cold wind spattering rain, past the black hills and the bare black sticks of trees and the two burnt towns before ours with their flat spaces and wreckage where houses had been. Leaning telegraph poles smouldered, and road posts, each with a red and a white eye melted like wax. Against the smoke over our town a yellow helicopter shuttled with its bucket of sea water on a rope.

The house was locked. Joan and Sam weren't there. I knew something was wrong then. It took me a while to find out where they were. Up at the hospital I saw Joan (she was still asleep) and identified Sam's body. It was Sam under the blanket. I said not to let Joan ever see that. She insisted, though; Marie told me.

Jake was there, Marie's man, black and weary after fighting the fire all night. He came up with me to their place. Half the houses on the hill were gone: nothing left but chimneys and strips and twists of corrugated iron buckled like cardboard and dumped over the rubble and ashes. At their place, glass that had melted lay in the yard in gobs like grey toffee. Rolls of black chicken-wire had been bedsteads. The garden was black stumps and tufts of smoke, a small flare in the gully, pale red-gold. The burnt tree lay where it fell. They had dug under it to get Sam out.

The opposite hill that had been thick bush was white with ash like a fall of snow. Walking over there we stumbled on mounds of flesh, torn already and loud with flies, as black as if they were mummified. A wombat, a few possums, somebody's cocker spaniel were still alive, burnt to the bone but still alive, and so we bashed their brains out. There must have been crows around, but I remember it as total silence. Silence and absence and bitter cold, as if the ash had been real snow.

We had a short service at the church, to which Sam's teachers and all the third grade came. We buried him in the cemetery on the hill. Bit by bit we gave his belongings away. We talked about living somewhere else, in or near Moorong, and perhaps we should have, but it seemed important at the time to try to go on living as normally as we could. I drove to school in Moorong and back every day. Joan worked her usual evenings at the hotel and I ate with her there after work and drove her home. She took an art class up at the school a couple of mornings a week: she wanted to drop that, but Marie talked her out of it. (Marie was – is – a teacher at the school.)

'The kids only want to do fire paintings,' Joan said. 'It's all they think about.'

'Maybe you should too,' I said.

'I don't feel like it.'

'Once you started –'

'I couldn't care less if I never paint again.'

She did keep on with the classes all the same. It was impossible to know what she felt. She always was like that, self-contained and solitary, careful to restrain her feelings. Except that she wore black every day now, and had lost interest in her painting, most of the time she might not have been bereaved. That was more than I could stand.

I hurt her, I suppose: I had to break through her silence.

'Talk to me, Joan, for God's sake,' I said in bed one night. 'Stop shutting me out. I've lost him too.'

'He was my child though. It's different.'

I was angry. Even in the dark she knew that.

'You'd like to blame me,' she went on. 'Say it then, why don't you: I should have made him stay with me.'

'You couldn't have known, nobody could.'

'*You* could have driven the long way round, if it comes to that.'

'I said I would. *You* said not to.'

'You didn't really want to, that's why!'

'I did want to.'

'But you didn't bother, did you?' And she ran sobbing out of the house. It was no use searching in the dark. I went back to bed and lay awake. She could have gone any-where. There was a moon that we'd watched sway up out of the sea, heavy, full, a deep orange. High and white now above the tree at the window, it drew on the wall the precise shadow of branches, every twig and leaf sharp.

I never asked and never heard where she went. It was the first of several nights. I imagine her at the cemetery or the Cascades, or tapping on a window somewhere; tapping on some man's window.

I went out into the garden: dew and silence underfoot, like a night in snow. The houses all had dark windows. The sea was flat, no sound of surf. Beyond its rim the lights of two squid boats, thrown up to a bar of cloud, stared landward like white-browed eyes. I went back to bed.

She came back a long time later and bedded down in Sam's room – the first of many times that she slept there. I never knew when she would, or why either. Other times she clung to me all night. Sometimes we made love. Both of us woke a lot, whimpering and clenched, having had a bad dream. She wouldn't talk about her dreams.

'He was driving me mad, he wouldn't stop talking,' she woke and said aloud one night. 'I let him go to Marie's. I couldn't wait to get rid of him.' I held her. 'He lay there watching them leave him.'

'Don't. I love you,' I said, too sleepy to think what to say, and she pushed me off wearily.

'Oh, *love* – what good's *that*? Oh, leave me alone. Go back to sleep.'

I couldn't. I touched her and she turned away.

I remember one time. I woke to find her shaking me gently and murmuring, 'Wake up. It's a dream. Wake up.'

'You were in it,' I said, and at once she turned on to her back. 'I'd come in and the house was stripped. Even the plaster walls were gone, and the bath, the sink, the basin, the linoleum. There was one tap dripping on to the dust. You were bringing Sam. We were all going out somewhere. I hugged you and him, but as soon as we walked out into the sun he faded into dots and stripes like a badly tuned television. I said, "I can't see him. I can see right through him." You said he was there all right. "He's *not*," I –'

'Stop it. I don't want to hear it.'

I lay still for a while. '"I don't want to hear it," that's you all right.'

'I have dreams too,' she said.

'Well, let's hear them! That's all I'm asking.'

She lay still. 'It makes me sick,' she said at last, 'the way you trot out your dreams as if you'd produced something *clever*.'

'That's what you think, is it?'

'I can't stand it. That's all. I can only take so much. You just have to leave me alone.'

'I thought we were together,' I said.

'We are. So far, anyway. Okay?' She turned her back.

I might have been strong enough for her, but for my own sorrow. As it was, we both started drinking heavily, apart and together: red wine for preference, in those days. Drunk, we could communicate or at least fight openly. (Friends began to avoid us.) In between times her silences went deeper. Silence, absence, a slow dissolution of the self: she was, I thought bitterly, as lost to me as Sam.

Then the rains came and we went to the Cascades.

The tail–end of an easterly was blowing the one time that I've made it back to our town since the flood. (The other times I've tried, I've turned back at Moorong.) I planned it well ahead and rented a car nothing like my own so no one would notice I was back in town. I was going to drive past our old place, and Marie's new one; and then keep well away from the centre.

Most of all since I moved to Melbourne I miss the easterlies, cold white easterlies of the coast sweeping up out of a white sky, a white ocean, and hurling froth over the beach. They blow for a week or more, summer and winter. Your hair goes stiff, your skin prickles from the salt. The seaward windows all over town film over. Perspectives flatten, as in fog or at sunset, warp as you look, so that the surrounding hills close in and hang over your head.

On the night of the fires the hills hung close like that, I've heard, as close as the rooftops.

I was ready for the first sight of the lighthouse on its bare headland. Then I saw the white surf and the long dunes, and all the tea-tree dead and leafless on them like black coral. In the first town and the second, new houses had been built and the raw wooden frames of others were up. Soft in the spray, the folded hills were a sweeter green than ever, sheep were ambling sunk in grass. There was a wide concrete bridge where the old wooden one had burnt down. Most of the charred gums still had life in them: they had covered themselves with a shaggy cape of lush green that looked more like ivy than gum leaves and left the crowns bare. Their wiry black tufts poked into the sky.

I drove into town along the back streets, keeping my head down. There were lights on already in the new pinewood house they had built on Marie's land. Heads in her front window rushed past me as I drove downhill. I should go to the Cascades, I thought. Now that I was here I couldn't remember what I had wanted myself to do. I went to the cemetery.

From up there in the wind you can see most of the town and the white ocean all the way back to the lighthouse: the houses, some new, and the flat spaces, and the black trees huddled in thick new leaves, all in a roar of wind and water.

A few of the old graves have sunk and the mud has coffin shapes embedded in it. The crosses on the mounds are askew and mostly illegible. The marble and cement of gravestones a century old has cracked under the shells and the plastic flowers: Joan's family name is on some of them.

I walked the long way round to Sam's grave, a mound with no name on it, only opal ear-shells and pebbles like white eggs. Someone (Marie, I think it was) had planted flowers in the middle, freesias, grape-hyacinths, bluebells.

It was true what I had thought I remembered: trains in the distance can sound like surf.

It was too public to stay long. I picked two freesias to take home. (I put them in water when I got back to the flat, and the next morning a brown spider was hanging on a thread between them, a spider from our town.) Then I drove to the edge of the rainforest.

Here out of the wind was a dank stillness. New tree-ferns like baby carrots were sprouting up under scorched old ones; others had fronds unscrolling, like green hands holding yoyos. New bracken hid the wet black fallen trunks of trees. I was the man sitting on a stump waiting for night to fall to make his escape. He knew there was nowhere he wanted to live but in this town, if he wanted to live. As far as he was concerned, though, it might as well still have been ringed with fire.

Long after the day of the fires the bush smouldered on. In the valley behind the coast, the open-cut coal mine poured towers of smoke up. People walking miles away would find themselves on a hot crust of earth, how thick no one knew: fires were burning underground, along veins of the coal. When the rains came five weeks later, people driving at night into the town through the burnt hills saw through their streaming windscreens a glow of red here and there where trees were still burning.

Fleshy belladonna lilies were the first plants to grow out of the ash. Then grass sprouted at the roadsides, so bright that it looked like a corruption – mould on rotting matter, algae on ponds. Inland the hills stayed bare, but along the coast the green haze thickened by the day.

Close to shore the sea went dark with burnt leaves; the sand was scribbled along every tide mark with a charcoal line of leaves, and littered with black trunks lashed around with kelp.

On the day of the flood, however, the sea was grey, thick with the earth and ashes that the rivers were gouging out. I had to miss school. Burnt trees loosened by the rain had fallen and blocked the back road out of town and on the coast road the gravel ford where the bridge had burnt down was feet underwater; on the third road, the long way round, landslides were expected.

We stayed in bed most of the morning and for once we were close and gentle with each other, though nothing much was said. After lunch I was restless. I wanted to go and see the river. Joan didn't, she said, but I was feeling reprieved, overjoyed: I couldn't part from her. It would do her good. Didn't she love walks in the bush? She gave in. We walked hand in hand along the beach in the thick rain, then up the swilling river-path, our boots bogging in the silt, and past the quarry to the Cascades.

I remember that the quarry dog was howling.

Two forks of the river meet at the Cascades. On the far bank the trees were black, their leaves scorched rusty brown, but the fire had not touched the trees on the other bank. Between them, the living trees and the dead, two grey spouts of water joined with a smash like surf breaking. As we watched, a whole black tree hurtled downstream and, rolling and frothing, rammed itself against a high rock.

'I'm wet *through*,' she shouted. 'Let's go *home*!'

The loose rocks we had crossed were already under-water: we would have to clamber up the bank to where the path led uphill. I went ahead, clutching at roots, slipping flat in the mud more than once and swearing. She didn't make a sound. Even in the roar of the water I think I would have heard. (*I can't remember*.) All I know is that when I turned round at the top I saw her – it was Sam's yellow raincoat that she had on – I saw her flying down the long, deep slopes of water that the Cascades had become.

I slithered down, ran and waded to the yellow bubble of the raincoat. She had been trapped where the dead tree was still wallowing in froth and tearing its black bark off in strips, thudding against the rocks. I screamed, 'Joan!' Our eyes met. A torn branch snapped and the tree rolled. Abruptly she sat up with the jackknife twitch of a corpse undergoing cremation. Then she was under the grey water.

I plunged in, sank, swam until I found footholds, and lost them again until at last I wrenched her free and into still water and on to the bank. Too exhausted to lift her, I had to pull her like some black log up on to the firmer mud. I loosened the clothes at her throat and, clutching her by the hair, pressed my mouth over hers and sucked, blew, sucked, blew, sucked. She didn't breathe. It was a long time, I think – I was half-drowned myself – before an old woman from the caravan park found us and went for help. Perhaps Joan was unconscious, perhaps dead, even as she reared up. In any case she was dead when help came.

Her blood was rusty in my mouth. The raincoat was still spreadeagled on the tree: I can see the yellow dance of it.

Though I stayed on at the school in Moorong till the end of first term, I hardly remember anything about it. I sold our house – an old weatherboard looking east over the ocean – easily and for more than I expected. I was thought to have left town long before I did: few of the locals ever saw me. Some of them might have taken that as an admission of guilt. Very soon, I suspect, I was a town legend. There are several. There's the old bloke in the fish story, for one. He gets home from the pier with a bucket of live salmon trout only to find his wife in bed with a neighbour. The neighbour takes off out the window and the old bloke, bellowing his rage and anguish, grabs a trout and shoves it headfirst up her cunt. Well, I'm the young bloke who not only lets his kid get trapped by a tree in the fires, he has to let another one drown his wife. It has that touch of the grotesque that makes a legend.

Some of the locals were good to me. Marie was. Since the fires she and the boys, and Jake sometimes, had been spending a lot of time at our place, now and then staying the night. (They were living in a borrowed caravan.) She came now as well, and stayed. What the locals couldn't take was the thought of Marie and me. That put them right against me.

In flashes of memory from time to time I confuse Marie with Joan. Not that Marie was a stand-in during those last few weeks. She knew that.

It was good to lie along her back with my arm round her shoulder, her breath a warmth that came and went on my open hand. Often I stayed awake. Hours would pass while I looked at the branches on the wall and held this warm woman in her sleep or she held me. Once when I got up and went walking round in the garden she came out – I saw her moving towards me in the white light – she came and put her arms round me, and we went back inside and lay down again. The surf was loud in the room.

I lay in her arms and told her what I had been dreaming about: the lava, the gully of burning bracken. She listened patiently. I came to the boy asleep at the core of the fire.

'*Don't*,' she said, twisting away, and I remembered.

'I'm sorry.' Her face under her hands was hot and wet. 'I didn't mean it.' I turned her round to me. It was pure thoughtlessness. I had forgotten for the moment who she was. When we were calmer she told me that Joan had seen Sam's body. That was the first I knew. They went in together, Joan and Marie, and had a look under the blanket.

At daybreak, I remember – shrill birds in the leaves at the window – we were awake, naked, and Marie took a firm hold of my cock suddenly.

'You're a tower of ssh,' she murmured into my mouth.

'Strength?'

'Flesh. Your tower of flesh. All right, strength.'

A tower of strength. To think that she was looking to me for strength.

It was because of Sam that she was with me; but he was always between us too. Not that we talked about him much, or Joan either: it was mostly about our pasts and our futures. All the same, he was there. When her boys started staying overnight (they'd been having skin grafts at the hospital in Moorong), I couldn't bring myself to say they could have Sam's room. It was full of boxes of books, I said, and put them on camp beds in the sleepout. She must have known, and been hurt. Besides, there was Jake as well. She and Jake were in the same morass that Joan and I had been in since the fires, and he was seeing other women even before that. Still, I knew that Marie didn't take seriously the thought of any future without Jake. She was marking time.

We didn't break off abruptly. Before the final settlement at ninety days Marie moved into my place and looked after it while I shuttled between there and the flat. The new owners let her rent it from them while her house was being built. She was the only person in town who knew the address of this flat.

She wrote at Christmas. The boys were well again. Jake was back 'for now': she sounded off-hand about it, so as not to hurt me, I suppose. I answered that letter, but not the next couple. No more came.

I only rent this flat, and the house money is all in the

bank, I can live on the interest. It's just as well, since I'm in poor shape, getting by on fruit, cheese, vodka. I can't see myself ever teaching again.

While I was packing I went into Joan's shed for the first time since the fires, not expecting to find anything there: bundled in newspaper were photographs, enlargements and sketches, dozens of sketches, of burnt wallabies and possums. It must have taken her days out on the hills to find so many.

She had done a painting too and scrawled in red along the bottom of it: Firebirds. Birds flapped on a dark ground, their wings alight, some without legs, some with charred stumps and white bones protruding.

I remembered someone at the hotel one night saying that he'd had to shoot his dog after he'd found it with its legs burnt off; and Joan asking if anyone knew a legend about a race of legless birds that have to live the whole of their lives in the air, or had she dreamt it. I was shocked, for Sam's sake – though I still didn't know she'd seen him – and for the man's. I thought she was being morbid in a repellently sentimental way. Seeing my anger, she clammed up.

I had Firebirds hanging on the wall for a day or two. Marie saw it. Perhaps I should have left it for her. I had to take it down and put it away. I understand better now.

I stayed up the last night at the house, checking that I had packed everything I needed and then sitting by the window looking through Joan's photographs and sketches in the lamplight. A blue morning came up, sunlight like gingery water lapping at the pane. I touched my face to the cold glass and the skin froze on the bone. The lamp, alive all night, had turned yellow and dry like a leaf.

In a dream I have, Joan is being stalked by a tiger. I write down my dreams in the hope of finding the one detail, the variation, that will change the pattern of events or give me a new key to it. A barred white and gold tiger: that could be the fire, or the charred tree trunk, its bark flayed off in stripes. I am usually a boy, Joan is my mother. Am I Sam? (Sam-I-am: that was in a book Sam used to love.) I have tried to warn her, but her look as the tiger leaps always accuses me, as if she thinks I'm its master, I could call it off, but I stand and gloat. In this dream the only sound is of fire or water (they sound the same).

Joan was six years older than me.

I wait for an illumination. Months go by as I wait here unable to take up the burden of my life. Doubts torture me. What look was that in her eyes? Could she have believed I was willing to let her die – stand by and let her die? Was she thinking that a death like that was what she deserved? What she wanted? Or that I thought so?

Some of the locals were sure of it. Joan's family was, especially after Marie moved in. It was a coroner's case, after all, since it was not from natural causes. An autopsy was done at the Moorong hospital and a report sent to the inquest. There was no talk of laying charges. The local sergeant was someone who had known us both for years. He took a statement from me the day after, and he and a constable went carefully over the ground taking photos and measurements. There were no suspicious circumstances, no prima facie evidence, as they put it: the inquest was a formality. That was just as well for me, I suppose, juries being what they are. (They're holding an inquest, aren't they? some people said. That speaks for itself. Well, doesn't it?) I got through all this somehow. My mind recoils from the effort of remembering it in any detail, let alone the thought of what a court case would have been like. The finding, anyway, was accidental death: she drowned after falling into the Skye river while it was in flood. Her head injuries and lacerations were not severe, according to the pathologist's report. The brain was not damaged.

He also reported that she was pregnant – about three months, evidently. Which document I saw this written on I can't remember. (If I can't trust my own mind, what foothold have I?) I do remember I asked a doctor friend if the pathologist could be mistaken; he only looked at me in consternation and (I think) pity. Later I asked Marie if she'd known. 'No,' she said, 'she hadn't said a word. You mean she hadn't told *you*?' she cried out. 'Oh. Peter.'

Anonymous letters arrived in the mail, made up of words cut out of newspapers and pasted on black paper:

YOU MURDERED HER YOU DROWNED HER IN COLD BLOOD

YOU WANTED THE BOTH OF THEM OUT OF THE WAY DIDN'T YOU YOU MURDERER

YOU DRANK HER BLOOD IT WAS ALL OVER YOUR MOUTH

YOU THINK YOU GOT WHAT YOU WANTED WELL HER ASHES WILL BURY YOU IN THE END (Her will – we made our wills when we bought the house – said that she was to be cremated. Her ashes are in Sam's grave.) Ludicrous letters, insane of course, but they harped on my doubts. Had I hesitated for a second at the Cascades? Couldn't I be bothered, honestly, to come home on the night of the fires? I know the mind can keep its secrets from itself. But if I know anything, I know I wanted her to live and Sam to live. If I can know anything. (Did I know Joan?)

I showed Marie one of the letters. 'I've got one of those,' she said. But she'd burnt it.

'What did it say?'

'Oh. About Sam. Us. You can imagine the sort of spiteful bullshit.'

'Any idea who it is?'

She only shrugged.

Beyond the doubt of myself I have a worse doubt, because the coincidence is so obvious, and not only to me. If I could be sure that their two deaths grotesquely mirror each other by blind chance, well and good. I could take up my life again, abandon myself to the flux, to chaos. But what if it is as it seems, a maniacal joke? And our story seems to make clear that I was instrumental in their deaths. If so, the hand that wielded me as the instrument wished us ill. (The floods were God's tears, one old woman said.) We are set in motion by a malevolent hand, unable to know in what our actions are rooted or what fruit they will bear. Why are we?

Rather than bring harm to anyone else, let me remain suspended out of life, of time, beyond all possibility of action.

Sometimes I go to the local library to read for a while in the warmth. I walk round the streets, drive to a beach now and then for a spot of fishing off the pier. I like sitting in churches and in public bars, quiet ones with an open fire. No one disturbs me. I have nothing to say to anyone there.

The days are long, though drawing short again for the second winter. More and more are dark with rain, soft rain. Here it leaves no salt on the lips. I spend more mornings than I can count sitting up in bed in the sun with a glass of vodka and a pen and white sheets of paper. Trains trundle past. The sun catching my fingers through the paper fills them with a milky red light. I make disjointed notes:

The pines shelter a green shade on the foreshore. The wind shifts: a quick shine on the needles of the marram grass and the spider threads between them.

Red wine has the rusty taste of blood. Vodka tastes of nothing, not even itself.

If I write our story, then will it give up its secret?

MARINA

THE LAST light flowed in and lapped around the baby asleep in the bassinette, fingers waving like stalks of seaweed. The ginger cat, waking, stretched and licked and came to rub its pelt against Marina's ankles. With her foot Marina tapped the crusted saucer of milk. Its bold yellow eyes fixed, the cat yowled and scratched at the linoleum. She shoved it out and slammed the door.

She thought, I'm afraid all the time. Of faces. Interiors, dreams. Voices. Pain. Dreams most of all.

In the shawl that Michali's mother had sent, with the blue bead sewn on it against the Evil Eye, the puffy head was haloed. Hairs tufted it. She touched the milk blisters on its lips, the red blotches on its forehead and eyelids, and watched it flinch under her shadow and grope with monkey paws. Her nipples stung. Her eyes burned with tears. This was all she had to show for the long pain and terror of giving birth; the ache of the stitches between her legs; the brown trickle of blood.

She could hear the baby's breathing and her own. The sun ebbed away. She sat waiting.

In one dream, she thought, a brittle glittering cockroach crawls out from under my thumbnail. Its eyes and wild feelers thrust against my fingers as I prod it back in. More cockroaches sprout from under each bitten fingernail. What do dreams mean?

A grey web was spun across the pane. A grey lair, a crouching spider. The brown sun pierced it. Clouds blew

125

loose on the square wan sky. Paint peeled in grey hang-nails from the spouting and the furrowed weatherboards. Hanging raindrops glittered, dripped down. A bird hooted.

Michali was needed at the pizza bar until just on mid-night. He would lurch in drunk and say, Go to buggery the pair of you, you shit me. When she first started work-ing there, he talked like that to his wife Joss. On the sly he kissed Marina. He said he loved her.

A black blowfly was squatting on the baby's cheek. It came out of its nose, or its mouth, or its curled ear. Marina waved it into the air.

She had written to Michali's mother. It must have got to Greece by now, but it might take Michali's mother weeks to answer. If only she could come and help. Even little Eleni had been led off, red and baulking, to stay at the pizza bar with her aunt. It's my baby too, Daddy, why can't I stay and help Rina? Mama, Marina thought, you can't come to Australia. I wish I never had. My own mother hates me. I must get to a good doctor. Michali doesn't believe me. I must find another doctor or something ter-rible will happen. I can't take the valium, it would get in my milk. I won't wean it, I want to feed it myself.

Dear Mama, she had written. Michali's mother was *Mama* now. Her own mother hated her.

Dear Mama,

Please write soon. Do you mind that it's another grand-daughter? I know Michali wanted a boy. He has taken Eleni to the shop because I just can't manage. I'm not working there any more. Eleni wants to be godmother, I suppose five is old enough. We're calling it Anna. People are saying we should call it Olga after my mother, but why should we? She wishes I was dead. She came to the hospital to look at the baby and went home without seeing me. A Greek nurse told me. We should have stayed in Greece. I told Michali.

I wish this one could have been called Eleni too, after you.

I have plenty of milk. Why does it vomit and cry so much, Mama? Tell me what to do. I'm afraid to sleep, I have such

terrible dreams. You'd know what they mean. Write to me
soon, please write.

Your loving daughter-in-law,
Marina

I often dream that I am hiding behind the dark curtain in
my parents' bedroom watching my mother go out. I
advance to the pane. My mother outside is watching me,
advancing on her own face printed in sunlight on the glass.
Her golden mask obliterates mind. Mine. I watch her raise
her black bag and bring it down, shattering the thick pane:
glass splashes me.

Marina lay down on the bed, twisting her hair into a
knot. The baby stirred and sucked in its sleep. Somewhere
a clock struck seven.

At seven the first morning in Michali's village his
mother burst in with green figs ripe to splitting, opened
the hot shutters and perched on their bed to peel figs for
her son and his *nyfi*. Don't come bursting in like that,
Mama, Michali said, if you want us to make you a grandson. When he laughed, pink seeds oozed from his mouth.
The whitewashed house was hot and sour, full of grapes in
baskets.

On burning afternoons Michali's mother bathed various
grandchildren one by one, sitting Laki, Niki, Eleni in the
brimming copper tub under the grapevine, soaping them
and rinsing off the bubbles with her tin watering can.

Eleni still clung to Marina. In the cool of dusk Marina
humped her round the village to buy icecreams at the
petrol station. Voices called from a walled garden: *Ela,*
nyfi, na sas doume ligo. Coffee with opal bubbles was
brought under the shade of a pear tree, and conserves of
tomato and quince like red glass. All the cows came jog-
gling home in the dusty streets with swollen udders hitting
their mud-caked legs. Their eyes watched as their muzzles
plunged into buckets of water.

Was there a woman that Michali visited even then behind locked shutters? He said he was fishing in the river while they slept the afternoons away but he came back empty-handed mostly. I fell asleep, he said: they got away. There's this big old one I'm after and he knows it.

He was happy before the wedding and after. They all were. He was proud. Look at her, he said, she's all of eighteen (he was thirty). She speaks perfect English and Greek. He showed people photos of the pizza bar. It was years since he'd been home. Everyone soon found out that she was pregnant already and no one seemed to mind.

The nights when he was at the *kafeneion* with his old friends his mother sat crocheting the white shawl, her glasses low on her nose, and talked about Michali's boyhood. We should have stayed, Marina said into the dark air. I wanted to.

I told Michali. Find me a doctor who can help me.

She lit the wick afloat in a skin of oil on water at the base of the ikon, and the faces of the Panagia and the Child appeared behind its flame. Their eyes were heavy with sleep or sorrow. *Haire*, Maria. Marina crossed herself.

The priest at the wedding sprouted so much black hair that she thought the resonating cave of his mouth must be furred bushy black, but no, it was smooth; it was the colour of a sea urchin. For the first time in her life the smoke from the rings of candles and the incense filled her with nausea. Faces grinned. In the dome Christ Pantokrator stared. She swayed, numbly aware that she might faint, or vomit, or cry out. The glass of the chandelier splashed.

In another dream, Mama, I have fed the baby thick porridge. I knew I shouldn't, oh I knew it wasn't right. Its nose and mouth ooze porridge and it chokes. I see its little tongue roll lolling out to its scabbed navel, roll out like a paper party whistle.

In the brown stillness Marina jumped up and grabbed her handbag. She bent over the breathing baby. It was so quiet. There was an hour or so before it should wake for the next feed. Michali had to work late. He was seeing another woman. His hands were clamped on a red dress. Tell me what to do. The baby's cheek was hot. *Panagia mou*, watch over my child.

Quickly she switched on the lamp by the bassinette and crept outside, locking the front door. On the verandah she wavered: in the front bedroom window her shadow covered the glass.

The corner milk bar was drenched in white light. Newspapers lay yellowing in heaps, *Neos Kosmos*, *Nea Ellada*, inside the plate glass windows. In the back room a television set yelled and chuckled. Kyria Anna was behind the counter weighing out sweets for an old woman in a ginger coat.

'Kyria Anna, *kalispera*,' Marina blurted, 'I have to ring Greece. Can I use your phone? I've got the money.' She fumbled in her bag.

Kyria Anna flounced and shrugged, but she was too fond of Michali to say no outright to his wife. Marina sidled behind the counter, checked the number in the torn book and rang International Calls. She stuttered to the shrill operator, and hung up. There was only one telephone in Michali's village: his mother, called over the loudspeakers, would come running down the dusty road. Marina stood wringing her hands. The old woman smiled. A stench of urine rose from under her hairy coat. Sticks in loose stockings, an umbrella, grey straggles squashed under a beanie. Among her freckles and creases her bold yellow eyes peered.

The telephone rang.

'Hullo, Melbourne? Would you repeat your number, please. I'm sorry, the number you are calling is not answering.'

'Oh. Thank you,' Marina uttered. 'I might try later. Thank you.'

'Is anything the matter, Rina *mou*?' Kyria Anna's grey face glinted. She would report to Michali. The old woman chuckled, trudging out.

'No, no. I'm fine.' Marina's head throbbed. 'They must all be out in the fields.'

'Well, never mind. You can always have another try. Sit down and keep me company for a while.'

'Isn't Elly home?'

Daughters like Elly were never home. Kyria Anna sighed complacently. Ach, *aman*. The thought rose into Marina's mind that it was Elly with Michali the other day in the half-dark of the cobbled yard. The black hair, the body draped in red. Elly, of course. Pain and anger surged in her.

'Tired, Rina? You look tired. Let me get you a little coffee.'

'No, thank you. No. I can't stay.'

'*Ela*, Michali won't miss you for a minute or two.'

Kyria Anna knew very well when Michali worked late; they had been neighbours for years. Marina glared into her pouched old eyes.

'No, I'd better not. Isn't Elly in, Kyria Anna?'

'No, dear. She had to go for a fitting.'

Kyria Anna was an old hand. Marina peered around the cluttered walls for mirrors and darkened panes to reveal to her how she looked to Kyria Anna. A dupe, parading her anguish and disorder. Brown hair falling in wisps, damp patches over her nipples, a draggled skirt. Long eyes slit against dazzle and suspicion.

'I really must go straight home.'

'*Kala*, *kala*. Come back and try again.'

'No. It's no use.'

Marina watched herself turn and sidle out in multiple faint images on glass. Lamps glittered over the grey street.

In another dream I have hurtled from an ivied window and lie crumpled on the cobbles in my white dress. Poor dead lady, look here she comes walking in the park with us in her wedding dress. Going upstairs to our warm bed we look back sorrowfully. She sleeps in her smashed carcase. The window strikes eight. Dreams will drive me mad.

At St Kilda beach the boats were rocking on the ruffles of the bay. Seaweed lay over the rocks to dry like calfskins. Gulls mewed and splashed. The pier lamps sank deep: men were fishing under them, crouched to fumble with white-bait, their long lines dipped in the eddies of light. One wound in a line with a pewter fish hung on it. Eleni, running up and down here one night in summer: Rina and Daddy! Come here! I want you emergently!

What is it?

Look! That man's caught a fish.

Ssh. That's the sinker.

It is not. It's a fish. It's very little, isn't it? Are you going to eat that little fish?

It's a fair size for one a these, missy.

Why don't you throw it back?

Shadows hid Marina on the ribbed wood of the landing stage. The piles under the jetty were shaggy with weed and mussels. She stood on a mess of crunched whitebait, and shuddered. The bay was fringed with lights under the heavy sky. As she watched, a shape of lights split from the lights of Princes Pier and drifted, a ship drifted out to sea.

The moon was rising, smeared with smoke or cloud.

She wandered on to the black sand. She was waist-deep in the water, hobbled by her long skirt, shoes in one hand. The waves glittered around her, the sand crumbled away under her feet. The cold water stung between her legs.

I am riding pillion on a motor-bike over a bumpy metal bridge, carrying the baby piggy-back. It falls off into the river. I see it lying on its back deep inside the clear water. I plunge my arms in and lift it up, but its head topples off and floats away. What can I do? Mama, tell me.

Marina heard that she was sobbing. Her mouth groped

and gaped. She tugged her wedding ring over her knuckles and hurled it glittering out to sea.

She strode through the water and up the sand to the street. Through the archway a flight of steps led to the Upper Esplanade. A tram clanked overhead. Leaves and papers littered the black steps. Here was where Michali had pushed her against the wall out of the jagged glare of the streetlamp and kissed her for the first time. A married man. The heavy gold of the asphalt by night. The smell of the flat sea.

Elly was there all the time, of course, in the back room of the milk bar watching the television. Elly and Michali were both there, furtive and bold, sneering at her.

In the moonlit air hung a vague smell, a dimness, an omen of smoke. Shivering, Marina broke barefoot into a clumsy run. Her skirt clung as she went pelting and gasping down the hot streets to fling the door open on silence, on a glow of lamplight. The baby stretched in its sleep.

The wick had dowsed itself in water furred with black insects. She poured more oil in and relit it. The faces shimmered. *Haire*, Maria. The insects would be burnt.

I had a doll that had been my mother's, with a china head on a cotton body. Dolly's head came off on the footpath. My mother took Dolly away and slapped me. She hates me.

Marina pulled off her wet clothes and put on dry ones. Her nursing pads stuck, yellow-crusted with milk. There were napkins soaking in the outhouse. She sagged at the thought of washing them out in the concrete troughs under the bulb in its net of cobwebs.

Outside an owl hooted. In Greece owls were unlucky. Ominous birds. Village women refused to go outdoors at night when one was about. There had been one under the lamp at the crossroad near Michali's village, sitting with a golden gaze in the dust, ruffling away, if you came too close. A dowdy cat with wings, over the wheat fields.

Her cold feet clinging to the linoleum, she opened the

refrigerator: olives, hard-boiled eggs, tomatoes; slices of old *tiropita*, dried cheese in curls of pastry; a bottle of milk, cold and thick, not like her own blue milk warm in her breasts; wooden yellow apples. She ate everything with both hands.

The baby slept on and on, breathing deeply. It would stay awake the whole night now.

Michali, coming home drunk the other night, had found the baby awake, shrieking – Eleni hovering pale and anxious – and yelled that the place was a madhouse and stank of shit. He staggered to the toilet and hugged the bowl, his chin on the rim. Vomit burst into the water. She wiped his loose mouth and dragged him along to the separate room that he had slept in for the last two months – driven out, he complained, by her thumping belly and her moaning when the cramps clutched her legs. She peeled off his sodden clothes and tucked him into bed. His breathing was slow, heavy. She flushed the toilet.

What the hell's wrong with you anyway, Rina? My brother's got three kids. His wife can help us out in the shop. Why not you?

His first wife, Joss, was smart and efficient, but she drove right off an overpass at the end of the West Gate Bridge. She had passed safely over the towers of factories, the still white tufts of steam torn from them, ships at berth, clouds hanging. In the dim mass of the city all the lamps were coming on. The sun glared on sheets of rainwater mirroring sky and clouds. Dazed, surging past, Joss had been crushed at full speed.

Michali had never loved Joss. He had often said so. It had only been a civil wedding. Her Greek was hopeless. Why had he married her? Because of Eleni? Marina had been ill with remorse for having wished Joss out of the way. The other day behind the crates of bottles Michali had been kissing someone, Elly. Marina had faded into the passage. It was Elly's turn now, Elly he entered with a groan and prodded and hammered. Elly could have him.

They were both – they were bestial.

A whimper echoed in the lamplight. The baby began its squalling. Its napkin was soaked with mustardy excrement; pimples studded its buttocks. She dabbed methylated spirit on the rash, as the Sister had advised, while it screamed under her hands. She should bath it, but she shrank from its panic, its slithering body dripping soap. In her desperation she stepped back, tipping over the cat's saucer. Sour milk splashed her foot and lay curdled on the floor.

She picked up the baby, sat down, dragged her jumper up and shoved the bawling head at one tight nipple. It shrieked. Its frilled gums grinned.

'Stop it!' she shrieked back. 'What's wrong with you? *Stop it.*' She grasped the baby's feet in both hands and swung it with all her strength head–first against the wall. And again. And again.

Then it stopped its noise, hanging from her hands.

She cradled the head. Blood trickling from the nose was staining the cheeks so she wiped them and kissed them and held the lips to her nipple. With a sweet sting her milk let down. Ah, she sat back and the white spray fell quietly in the baby's face.

A GIRL ON THE SAND

I THINK I could live in almost any country now so long as I was not beyond the range of seagulls and the smell of water, salt water, lifted in on the wind.

'We Greeks, we can make a life in any country, Dimitri,' I remember my mother insisting. We chose Australia because there was work, and we have made a life. We have more or less mastered the language. We are here to stay.

This part of the coast of Australia, facing Bass Strait and the Southern Ocean, is where I want to build a house when I can afford one. Not because it reminds me of Greece. Except in its wildness it hasn't the least resemblance to any part of Greece that I knew. Maybe the wildness is why. The village of my childhood was on the plains under a ledge of mountains. Thunderstorms along this coast have all the savagery of the ones I remember, when lightning bolts struck farmers down in the fields and fireballs burst in at windows and burned children in their beds.

We talk a lot at home about the storms, the floods and droughts and iron winters, what was done in the War and then the Civil War. We feel it proves what we are made of. I have heard Australians talk with the same pride in having endured. Our countries have barrenness in common: the centre of ours is jagged rock, the centre of Australia dry sand and rock, and we take pride in this even if we never set foot there. May your soil be barren, one of our great modern poets has written – I forget his exact words. May your soil be barren so you don't have room to spread roots and so you keep groping deep.

It must be every day of fifteen years since I came to Australia with my mother and my married sisters. After the first months at General Motors I've mostly worked in restaurants and hotel kitchens, studying part time in the last few years to get a science degree. All I need now is a Diploma of Education and my mother will have a teacher for a son. This will impel her to try even harder to find me a bride. I'm forty this year and one failed marriage is more than enough, I tell her. I left all thought of marriage behind in Greece.

I spend a lot of time in this town on the coast, in the water when I'm free during the day and fishing on the pier at night. A lot of us sit in a row on the planks with a crayfish boat on props towering over us on each side. (Two cranes on the pier lower the boats into the water and hoist them out again.) There are the lights of the town slithering over the water, and far across it the slow red flicker of the lighthouse. There is the creak and lap of water on wood, as if we were in a boat on calm water. It was like that, fishing from a *varka* with a lamp on the gulf at night, out of Thessaloniki. But the sea wasn't icy and wild like this sea, or not often.

If my family has found life full of harshness here, it hasn't been any more so than we were bred for.

This afternoon, the lunch rush over, the rest of the staff have gone across the road for a swim: I'm going as well as soon as I clean up. Too tired to hurry, I trudge round collecting the last cups with their saucers full of slops and sodden butts. The door handle jiggles. Someone is making wild signs against the blue glitter of the sea: Jake, a local, a friend I go fishing with, so I have to unlock the door.

'Jesus, Jim. *Jesus*.' He shakes his head. His face is yellow, his eyes wide.

'Cup of coffee?' I'm being offhand to make it clear that whatever has happened I'm not turning round to make him lunch at this time of the afternoon.

He nods. Sitting at a smeared table, he covers his face with tight hands while I make a strong short black for the both of us.

'Well?'

'I've been up at the police station.'

I wait. Jake's a journalist. He makes the most of the stories he has to tell.

'Well, I went round to Western River.' I know that; he asked me if I wanted to come. 'Went for a swim, fished off the rocks for a while, you know, time goes by.' He catches my look. 'Listen, you bastard. There'd been a quick shower, heavy for a moment but only enough to make pits in the sand and raise a hot smell. A rainbow was forming out at sea.' I know those rainbows stretched from cape to cape. 'I was looking at it and paddling back through the warm water along the edge of the river and so' – he takes a deep breath – 'I nearly trod on her before I saw she was there.'

'A woman?' A lot of Jake's stories involve a woman.

'She had her legs in the water, half in, half out. Wide apart. And not a stitch on. She was – white all over. Long black hair full of seaweed and things hopping, sandflies. Oh, Jesus.' He stirs his coffee and takes a gulp. 'She was white and sort of grainy like – I don't know – white sugar. Or sand, a sand sculpture, seaweed for hair. She had dark stains on her.'

'Was she dead?'

'Of course she bloody was.'

'There's a bit of a rip along there.'

'She was dead before she got into the water, it looks like. Or so the cops say.'

'Murdered.'

'That's what Bill reckons.' Bill, the local sergeant, is a friend of Jake's. 'Smothered or strangled. They'll have to have an autopsy. Can you manage another coffee, Jim?'

I take the cups to the machine. I know the spot he

means, where the river curves past a cliff of jagged brown rocks as bright as snakeskins. The cliffs that face the ocean at Western Beach are black, damp from noon on, and their shadows darken the sea at their base. I was fishing there just the other day. The high yellow slopes of scrub and autumn grass were heat-shaken. An undertone of insects would suddenly lurch close, sun-jewelled, then away out of sound. In the dark under the ocean cliffs the beach was as cold as a cave.

'She wasn't on the ocean beach?' I put down the coffees.

'Thanks. No, up the river a bit. The tide was going out.'

'You could tell she was dead.'

'Oh, Jesus, yes, right away. There was this sweetish – funny, though, I couldn't leave her there while I went and reported it. I don't know why. I couldn't bring myself to touch her – try to drag her up on to the sand or whatever. What if I gave her arm a tug and it came off in my hand? That's been known to happen. Anyway, in the end I dropped my shirt over her and got up on to the road and stopped the first local that came past – the new bloke from the fruit shop, it was – and told him to send the police. Then I went back and waited with her. Jesus. The silence.'

'How old was she? Roughly, I mean.'

'Fucked if I know, mate. I couldn't – Jesus, how are you supposed to tell?' He knits his fingers together and stares at them. 'Bill reckons about sixteen and they're pretty sure she was pregnant. She was bloody huge. I just thought she was bloated.'

'Blotted?' A word new to me.

'Swollen up, blown up?' His hands shape a dome over his belly. 'Corpses do at a certain stage. I couldn't tell you how long it takes. Ever seen one?'

'Yes, often. In 1941 when the Germans occupied Greece. I was only a boy. I can't remember how long it took them to – blot.'

'Bloat.'

'People died in their sleep then, side by side on the

footpaths. When I woke up there would be a head bent back further along the row. A mouth open on broken teeth, eyes rolled back. Rats ate the noses off live babies.'

'Jesus. I never saw her face, come to think of it. Her hair was all over it. Can I have one more coffee and then I'll go?' But as I get up to make it he grabs my wrist. 'Wait on. I haven't told you the worst thing yet, have I? Jesus. The fucking worst thing.'

'Wait till I get the coffee.'

I make one cup. When I bring it he is leaning into the corner with his head flung back so that nothing of his face shows but his trowel of ginger beard.

'Coffee.'

'Yeah. Thanks, mate.' The beard waggles.

'This worst thing.'

He heaves himself round with a sigh to face me: 'She only had one hand.'

'One –'

'Hand. Bitten off in the water, I thought. But then I got a better look after the cops arrived. Her arm ended smoothly at the wrist. It must have come off a long time ago. Maybe she was born like that.'

'Little buds of fingers on the end of her wrist,' I say.

'That's right.' He narrows his eyes. 'How did you know?'

I shrug. 'I've seen it before.' (Where have I?) 'Why is that the worst thing?'

'Fucked if I know. It just is.' He sips the coffee. 'Ah! Good one, Jim.' I've put whisky in it.

He has nothing more to say. Neither of us has. Once he has finished his coffee and driven off, I lock the door and walk down to the beach. No one knows yet that a girl has been found, nudged by yellow ripples of water and sand. Her legs were open in the shape of a gulf. *Kolpos* means gulf in Greek; it also means vagina, which shocks my Australian friends – a word like that all over the map. The sea froths over my feet and tugs and furrows the sand under them. I no longer feel like a swim. I walk round as far as the rocks on the point (something is rising like a bubble in water to the surface of my mind) and lie down on the sand.

Kitchens have been my life. Ploughed fields were meant to be, as they were for my father; but when he was away fighting in the War and the Civil War we had to move to the city for safety. We found two downstairs rooms in a tenement in the red–light district of Thessaloniki, not far from the railway station. We slept on the floor on *kilimia*, all five of us, I and my two sisters, our mother and our grandmother. What hope did the girls have of growing up chaste, I overheard our mother ask our grandmother one night: ours would be like all the other families where brothers dishonoured sisters and ended up pimping for them.

'What rubbish, Melpo,' my grandmother said. 'Dimitri's not like that. You know he has a sense of honour.'

A sense of honour: *philotimo*. Or rather, a pride in one's honour. Of all things to saddle me with. A very selective honour, since I stole, or we would have starved. Perhaps there's no honour free of paradox; no pride either.

In 1946 when I was twelve I started work as a kitchen and water boy in a *taverna* owned by a friend of my father's. All the *tavernes* had one or two boys who worked from the early morning until midnight with an hour off in the afternoon, their shaven heads cuffed for the smallest mistake. They could scrounge a living from tips and food scraps. My tips came from the girls in a couple of nearby hotels and in the brothel, when I took meals to their rooms. They were fond of me and tried to keep me talking. They passed the time making coffee and telling fortunes in the grounds, gossiping about pimps and raids and abortions, and who had fought over whose girlfriend in what hashish den, and who had syphilis or consumption.

My mother knew this was part of my job. She wept over me and made me swear not to dishonour the family.

I wonder why I'm remembering this, after all these years. Is it because a girl with only one hand has been thrown up on the beach? She had long black hair. Maybe she was Greek. This is the moment when the bubble rises to the surface and bursts. I remember who she was.

At about half past two one dusty yellow afternoon she sidled into the *taverna* and ordered a *pilafi* and a lemonade at the counter. Our customers were working men, on the railways mostly: women didn't eat there alone. I saw her glancing nervously around, though no one, after the first stare, was taking any notice. She was a stranger, a country girl judging by her clothes (my mother would have known exactly where from) and by her bundle too, her *bogos* of worn home-woven wool which she balanced on the chair beside her. She wore a white scarf over her hair, and white gloves, in all that heat. I brought her bread and a glass of water. When her meal was served she drank the lemonade in one gulp and with the fork in her gloved hand she scooped up all the yellow rice and then she scrubbed the oil off her plate with the bread. Then she called me to ask for more water.

After I'd brought it she called me again. '*Mikre*,' she said: little one. It was how everyone called us boys. I went over, wiping my hands on my apron and wondering what she wanted this time. She had paid the waiter already. The last customers were getting up to go. 'Tell me your name?' she said, and slipped a coin into my hand.

'Why?'

She smiled. 'It's awful, calling you "*mikre*."'

'His name's Dimitri,' grinned a waiter on his way past.

'Mine's Dimitroula,' she said to me. 'Strange, isn't it? The same name.'

I shrugged. What was she getting at?

'Have you worked here long?'

'Two years,' I muttered.

'Will you help me then?' I had to bend down to hear her. 'I don't know a soul in Thessaloniki. I only just got off the bus. Do you know if there's a very cheap hotel round here that's – you know – suitable for families?'

I knew one. She sat back in relief, her hands clasped, and I saw her face, broad and brown with heavy-lidded dark eyes and a full mouth with a mole at one corner: an *elia*, an olive, as it's called in Greek.

I explained that she would have to wait outside for me. We could all see her standing there in the sun, shading her eyes to glance in from time to time. My friends and enemies all thought it was a great joke. 'What does she see in you, Dimitri?' one said. 'Can't she wait till your voice has finished breaking?'

'Shut up,' I said. 'You've got it wrong. She's my cousin on my mother's side.' They gave a yell of joy. 'She is. It's years since we saw each other. She lives in – Katerini.'

'And what's her name, Dimitri?' The waiter opened his eyes wide.

'None of your business.' She had opened her eyes like that as she said her name: I didn't believe it was Dimitroula. I had said Dimitri and she had said the first name that came into her head.

'He can't remember!'

'He forgot to ask!'

'Dimitroula!' I squeaked, to a burst of applause.

'Get on with the job, come on,' the cook growled. But he crooned 'Dimitroula *mou*' under his foul breath the whole time I was scrubbing his pots and pans. 'You've got one hour,' he called as I rushed out, and raised another laugh.

Red-faced, I hoisted the girl's bundle over my shoulder and set off with her trotting beside me down the gravelled laneways to the Hotel Epiros.

'Epiros!' She made a face.

'Well, it's respectable. It's for families.'

'Yes, all right. It was just the name. My parents live there, in a village near Albania.'

I put down her bundle on the doorstep. 'I told them at work that you're from Katerini. I had to say something.'

'A lot further than that.'

'I *know*.' Did she think I didn't know Epiros was near Albania?

'No. Where I live is much further than Katerini. Skala – I live in Skala with my aunt. I haven't seen my parents since the Germans came.'

'Seven years!'

'That's right. I don't care. Neither do they. Now the *andartes* have taken over.'

'You'd have been conscripted! They're conscripting girls.' She shrugged. 'Skala where?' There are villages called Skala this or Skala that all over the coast of Greece. She bit her lip and looked down. 'All right, don't tell me then. Suit yourself.'

The manager came: he knew me. If she hadn't been with me she would never have got in, since she had no papers on her. He handed her key to me.

The passages of the Epiros were dingy and rank and had cockroaches. Piss glistened on the bathroom floor; on the enamel footplates and in the holes of the lavatories shit of various shades was clumped. A country girl would be used to worse, I knew. The air in her room was hot, striped with dusty yellow light. But the sheets on the bed were washed and starched and the blankets were old army ones, thin but solid. Families from the villages stayed there regularly: no one would molest her.

I dropped her bundle on the stiff blanket and she sank down beside it, her scarf slipping so that her hair fell along the pillow in a flow of black.

I opened the window and went to unfasten the shutters.

'No,' she said. 'Let's leave them shut.'

'I have to go,' I said.

'No, stay a minute. Don't go, Dimitri.'

I felt uncomfortable. She saw that I did, and sat up. 'I don't know a soul. What will I do?'

'I have to get back to work.'

'I have to find a doctor.'

'What's wrong with you?'

She 'gave a snort and her gloved hand shaped a dome over her belly.

'Ah,' I said as if I knew.

'Three months. I have to get rid of it.' *Na to petaxo* was what she said: to throw it away.

'Ah.' Now I knew. 'Can't you get married?'

Her nose reddened and her eyes spilled out tears which she wiped on her glove.

'I've got the money. My aunt gave me plenty. It has to be straight away. She said, "You come back in that condition and I'll stick a knife through it and you."'

I hid my shock. 'I think I can find out where there's a doctor.' The whores were certain to know a good one.

'Oh, can you? Can you really? When?'

'Tonight. I'll come and tell you on my way home.'

'Will you? You promise?'

'Of course I will.'

'Dimitri, my life's in your hands.'

'I *know*. I said, I promise.'

I worked hard that night at the *taverna*, spurred on by jeers about how tired I looked. I knew who I could ask: Lina, the one I liked best, the one who made the most fuss of me. She had a lame leg, and that may have been another reason. When I went to pick up her dinner dishes – there'd been no time earlier – I asked if she'd do me a favour.

'Anything, anything, my darling,' she said.

So I stammered it out: where did she think my mother's cousin from Katerini could get a safe abortion? Lina lit a cigarette. 'You bad boy!' She goggled her black-rimmed eyes at me.

'Come on, Linaki. This is serious.'

'I'll say it is. You're telling me.' She passed me the cigarette for a quick puff. 'You could always marry the poor thing.'

I choked the smoke out. 'It isn't *mine*!'

'You all say that,' she sighed. 'Don't I know it?' She shrugged at herself in the wavy mirror, grabbing the cigarette and blowing a fan of smoke at her dark face staring back. She was enjoying herself. She went on like this for some time. Time was short, so was my temper, and the more thwarted and sullen I became, the more she teased. But she wrote a name and address at last. I grabbed her dishes and turned to go, but she took them back, put them on the dressing table and demanded a kiss. Angrily I jammed my mouth on her blotched lips.

'I won't tell,' she said. 'You be sure to take good care of your little cousin.' She stroked my cheek. 'She's in for a bad time. I should know.'

I kissed her again, and I meant it.

I ran to the hotel after work and told Dimitroula. She looked distraught and I felt bad about leaving her alone, but I was dropping with tiredness by then and my mother, as I explained, always waited up. Early next morning before work I took her to the address, a shuttered upstairs surgery. She was lucky, the nurse said: the doctor would do it that very morning. I knew I had no hope of getting off work early, so I told Dimitroula she would have to find her own way back to the hotel, but I would come straight after work and see if she needed anything.

It was well after three when I knocked on her door and called softly. 'Come in,' I heard. The door was unlocked, though she had the shutters and the window closed. In the thick heat I made out her face, a paleness as it moved on the pillow and made a ripple in her long strands of hair.

'Something to eat,' I muttered, having at great risk – a boy sacked for thieving wouldn't get another job – smuggled out a lump of stewed meat and potato wrapped in a teatowel. I presented it: the red sauce had soaked through. She gasped and turned abruptly away, flinging her brown arm up over her eyes and I saw that for the first time she wasn't wearing her gloves and – I peered closer in the dimness – *her hand had been cut off.*

I screamed.

'Take that thing away,' she groaned. 'Oh, it's all over blood. It looks like a – take it away, I'll be sick.'

I put the teatowel of food down on the floor outside her room and shut the door quietly. Her voice was thick, she had been crying. She was again, but she patted the blanket for me to sit down.

'*Why did he cut your hand off?*'

She sobbed, or laughed, and rubbed her wrist against my thigh. 'Don't be silly,' she said. 'Oh, why did you have to see it? I didn't want you to.'

'No, let me see.' I stared as she turned her arm, plump and brown on the top and white underneath like a loaf of bread. Her veined wrist ended in five small buds.

'How did it happen?'

'I was born with it like this. That's why my mother wouldn't have anything to do with me. My father's sister said she'd have me and they send her money every summer for my keep.'

'The same aunt? The one in – Skala?'

'Yes. She's fond of me in her way.' She caught my look. 'Well, she brought me up. A deformed child that no one wanted.'

'She made you come here by yourself and find a doctor.'

'She's letting me go back. Not everyone would.'

'Do you want to? After what she said about the knife?'

'Where else can I go? My own mother didn't want me to

live.' Her eyes closed and tears ran into her ears and her loose hair. She whimpered something I didn't hear.

'Don't cry.'

'I'm worse than she is now. I've killed my baby.'

'They made you, though.'

'But I wanted to have it. You should have heard my aunt. "You're hard enough to marry off already," she said. I know that.' She held her arm up. 'Who wants a wife like this?'

'Can I feel it?'

She nodded. I touched the nodules with my long fingers: they felt like a baby's knuckles.

'It's not so terrible. It's only when you first –'

'There's more to it than that. Don't you understand?' She leaned forward and whispered: 'Why am I like this? How would you like to be my husband and have to wait nine months to see if the child was the same as me?' She watched me understand. '"No wonder he ran away," my aunt said. The father. She called me a whore.'

I'll bet! Just what my mother would say if it was one of my sisters. A silence fell. 'Did you love him?' I said at last.

'He didn't even know about the baby. And a lot of men are after me, you'll be surprised to know. Crippled or not.'

'You're not *crippled*.'

'He was different. He was a boy I've always known. We were at school together. He had big ideas about saving the world and feeding the poor and all that. He never said he was a Communist. I wouldn't have cared anyway. He left home a few weeks ago. He's in Epiros with the *andartes* now. He never told me anything. That's what his best friend said.'

'You haven't heard from him?'

'No one has. He's dead or as good as dead. The *andartes* are going to get wiped out. Don't you read the news-papers?'

I didn't. 'He might come back when it's over,' I said.

'And be shot? His father's waiting. And his brothers.'

'But you still love him.'

'No.'

'Because he's an *andartis*?'

'No, because he left like that without a word. Because he didn't trust me.'

'Why did you love him?' I was, I realize now, jealous of the boy.

'Why! Why does anyone?'

'I don't know.'

'You will.' She smiled, but her face crumpled and she was whimpering again. I stroked her hair. My hands must have stunk of the meat stew but she stayed still, her eyes closed. 'I'm tired,' she said, 'and my belly hurts.' The hair close to her head was soaked with sweat, the ends dry and feathery. I smoothed it back off her forehead until her breathing went heavy. Then I crept out.

A squeal, the snake dash of a grey body, brought me up short. A rat was crouched in the corner. It had mauled the teatowel with the meat. Sick with loathing, I kicked the ragged mess down the passage a long way from her door.

On my rounds that night I took a dinner to the Epiros for her (Epiros, where her lover had gone): they could dock the money out of my pay, I didn't care. I chose *yemista*, one pepper and two tomatoes stuffed with rice, since she liked rice; and a serving of bread and a bunch of yellow grapes. I stumbled on the gravel in the dark, and trudged along the dank passages half-afraid of what I might find. But a light was on inside and she opened the door herself. The one dirty bulb in the ceiling made yellow waves on the walls, leaving the furniture in the darkness.

'Did you sleep?' I asked sternly as she laid herself down on the bed.

'Yes, I feel better.' When she smiled her face was sleek and brown again. 'Oh, look how much you've brought! You'll have to help me eat it.'

I ate some rice to please her. She was slow but she finished it all and sopped the bread in the red oil and made me have a bite before eating that too. She lay carefully back with a sigh.

'Was it good?' I was eager for praise.

'You saved my life.' That was something the whores often said, but not the way she said it.

'It's nothing.'

'Here.' She took more drachmas than the dinner cost out of her purse and pressed them into my hand.

'No, it's all right! I'll pay.'

'Don't be silly, take it. My aunt gave me enough for my expenses. You have a family to support, haven't you? Put it in your pocket, go on.' I put it in my pocket. 'Have you got a girlfriend, Dimitri?'

'No,' I muttered. 'I'm only fourteen.'

'Is that all? You look older. I'm sixteen.'

'What a shame. You're too old for me.'

'What a shame. And you're good-looking too.' Her tone, her teasing smile: it was just what I needed. On such familiar ground I could relax. 'Don't go thinking I can't do things,' she went on. 'I can. I have a sort of leather strap that I wear on my wrist. I can cook, sew, knit, mend nets. I can embroider and use the loom. Anything.'

'You mean you've got your *proika* ready?' Even in those hard times some girls had managed to make sheets and woven blankets and clothes for their *proika*. My sisters hadn't.

'Everything. Why not?'

'Well, I can't marry for a long time,' I assured her. 'I have two unmarried sisters.'

'Bad luck.'

Traditionally the brothers have to wait until their sisters marry. A few years later, as it happened, I did marry before them. It caused a lot of bitterness in my family and gossip outside it. After ten years of murderous turmoil – war, disease, hunger – the grip of tradition had loosened.

149

Magda, the girl I was in so much of a hurry to have, was like Dimitroula to look at, broad-faced and full-lipped. She had no physical flaw. Not even a mole.

'Aren't you going to eat the grapes?' I had to go back to work. 'They're good. Very sweet.'

'I'm too full. I'll have them for breakfast.'

I put them on the dressing table. 'You're sure you'll be all right?'

'Yes. You have to be getting back.'

'I'd stay with you if I could.' I wanted to stay.

'I know. I'll be all right, don't worry. I'll be leaving in the morning.'

'Will you come past the *taverna* and say goodbye?'

'If you want.'

'Is it the Skala near Platamona?'

She smiled. 'No. It's another one. Bend down,' she said, 'and give me a kiss.' Balancing the dishes, I knelt and kissed the mole beside her mouth. She turned her head to kiss me on the mouth. 'Good night,' we both said. Her damp hair smelled of salt.

That night for all my tiredness I lay awake a long time listening to the four women who depended on me, two old and two young, breathing in the dark.

Next morning she looked in through the door of the *taverna* – I was keeping an eye out – and waited till I had a chance to come outside. She was scarved, gloved and her face was sombre. 'I should have died,' she said. 'I wish I had. Then I wouldn't have to go back.'

'You can always come and live here,' I said, sure even as I spoke that she would never want to come back here. 'I could find you a room.' I was about to lose her.

'How would I live? Or don't you know?' I did know. She kissed my cheek, smiled, and walked off with her bundle.

With the passing of time I suppose I fell in love with her, or with the thought of her. I relived every word, every look. If I saw a white scarf in the distance, it had to be hers (and it never was). In my daydreams she came to the *taverna*, only this time I stayed the two nights at the hotel to keep her company and on the second morning she told me she was never going back to Skala. I worried when I changed my job: where would she find me now? I made up scenes, chance meetings. I would be taking meals up to the whores one night, for example, and find her among them. Or she would pass me in the street one day with a man and a child, children, and know me, or not know me.

We were fated to meet again. I was certain of it.

In the village your family is your life, or it was in those days. I was too young then to understand how she felt. When my wife Magda was caught in the arms of a neighbour who was our mortal enemy, she ran away; and the dishonour to our family drove my mother to emigrate to Australia. Maybe Dimitroula escaped by coming here, if the authorities would let her in with only one hand. She might have run away to the city; she would be easy to trace, but her aunt would hardly bother. My feeling is that she stayed in Skala and endured the darting eyes of visitors and the chatter in the street that stopped as she came near and waited for her to move on. They all knew too much about her, but she was never one of them. They smiled and kept their distance. There's no Greek word for privacy, as it's understood in English – nor for intimacy, if it comes to that. There is for loneliness: *monaxia*.

To be Dimitroula and be confined to Skala, wherever it was! I can see her as the scarved woman posed to give depth to postcard photographs: walking by a white bell tower or against fishing boats mirrored in the shallows. I saw a lot of sea ports during my national service. She might have been any one of the women – if I ever happened on the right Skala – that I saw watering geraniums in kerosene tins, hanging up herbs to dry, mending a net in a doorway, seagulls at her feet. (Did she ever think of me?)

If I did see her again, neither of us knew it. Her story has long since lost any power to move me. It must be twenty-five years since it occurred to me to wonder if she was alive, if she was happy or not. Now our lives have crossed a second time – no, drawn close without touching, a second time. Lives with their roots not spread but sunk deep.

No tide of any ocean could have washed her round the world from Skala to Western River, I know that. Even if she was living on this coast, she's forty-two now, not sixteen, and the sergeant said the girl was sixteen. That's not the point. Whoever she turns out to have been, and whoever killed her and why, the girl that Jake found has nothing to do with me. The link is too fine and fragile.

Even if it is Dimitroula.

The police will call on the public to come forward with any information that might help them identify the body. Nothing I have to tell could do more than confuse them and raise false suspicions. (Even if it is Dimitroula.) For me to claim more part in her life than I have had would be to falsify it. My part has been to stand by once – now twice – and witness, and stay silent. Why this should be, who knows?

What do I know about her? She was a beautiful, lonely, passionate woman who took risks. They think she was also pregnant. She has died by violence and her death seems to be something I was meant to learn of. Maybe I was meant to find her body; I spend a lot of time round at Western River. She looked like white sugar, he said. Or sand. I spread hanks of hairy seaweed in a fan. With my palms I raise and smooth the shape of a breast out of the sand, a second breast and the high dome of a belly. I make her two arms and one hand. I spread her legs wide apart. Between them a gulf of sand was formed as the yellow river water sank away from her.

Surfers are riding past me in the green waves.

A Girl on the Sand

The rocks here on the point are blistered with sandy pools where the water is blood-hot. There are limpets and blue-black mussels and grape weed. A beaded net in a pool below a rock is the reflection of the sun's glitter on lichen on the rock. I measure the slowness of bubbles as they rise. A small flathead sways and noses under shadows. Puckering the pool, an insect trails over the sand its own magnified shadow ringed with bubbles of light in the precise form of a tea-tree flower. A limpet lifts its lid as water nudges it: the tide is coming in.

What part, I wonder, does free will play? I talk of honour and endurance and love.

MATRIMONIAL HOME

HE RANG an hour ago, so his wife is expecting him, or he would turn back. The verandah lamp is on for him, throwing lights and shadows like a fire behind the rainy branches and the black iron fence, and the door is propped half-open. The gate squeals as he shuts it. A black cat sprinkled with rain strolls past him into the house. Not knowing if he should knock or call or go straight in, he dawdles on the verandah. Among the branches gold fruits are hanging. He remembers the persimmon tree and fondles one, cold and glassy and squat, heavier than it looks. And not gold, it was the lamp, but as dark as a ripe apricot.

'Hullo.' Margaret, in shadow by the door.

'Hullo!' He turns with a stiff smile.

'You're wet.'

'*Il pleut doucement sur la ville,*' he recites.

'I know how you hate the rain. Well, come in.'

'I was just admiring the persimmon tree.'

'Yes, it's never had so many. You must take some home with you.'

'Home.'

'Doesn't Sandra like them?'

'I told you. I'm at my sister's.'

'Your sister loves them.' She waits for him to follow her in and latches the door.

'No wonder Annie called it the Persimmon Tree House,' he says, for something to say.

'What did you say?'

'Annie. The Persimmon Tree House.'

A log fire burning gives the sittingroom its only light. In front of it the wet cat sprawls and preens its belly. It makes a smudge of black among flames that the floorboards mirror.

'Oh,' his wife says. 'When she was little. We don't call it that any more,' she adds after a moment.

'Why not?'

'It's the Matrimonial Home these days.'

'I wrote to the solicitors, Marg. I told them to call it off.'

'They wrote, yes.'

'You know I don't want the divorce.'

'It was the marriage you didn't want the last time I saw you. Now it's the divorce. No pleasing you, is there.'

'I wasn't really expecting to be welcomed with open arms.'

'I wouldn't put it past you.' She takes his sodden coat and hangs it up. 'Come and sit down.'

He sinks into the velvet chair that used to be his, spreads his legs out to the fire, lights a cigarette. Blinking scornfully, the cat jumps up and sniffs the seat of the other velvet chair, but his wife pushes it off.

'New cat.' He hates cats. She knows he does.

'He was a consolation present. He has a nasty nature but he's beautiful, or the other way round.' She feels awkward too. 'Coffee, or wine? You have had dinner?'

'Yes, thanks. Sorry, I meant to bring a bottle.'

'No need. These are yours. There's a chardonnay in the fridge, or there's red. French, or are you tired of French wines? There's some Napa Valley red.'

'The chardonnay, please. I'll open it.'

'No you won't. I will.'

He laughs. 'Why?'

'I can fend for myself. You're my guest. Not that you're not legally entitled to be in the Matrimonial Home, if it comes to that. I assume it won't tonight.'

'Margie, don't.'

'I'm behaving badly.'

'I deserve it.'

He stands by the fire until she comes back and pours green-yellow wine into two glasses.

'Cheers.' He raises his glass.

'Cheers. Well, welcome back. I thought the idea was to stay in America till June.'

'I wound things up earlier. I just had to get back by Easter. I wrote to you about all –'

'Yes, I got it.'

'Oh.'

'I started to answer it but I tore it up. It seemed more sensible to wait and see, considering.'

'Considering?'

'How much your letter didn't say.' A log shifts, covering itself in eddies of flame, and cuts off what she is saying next. For the first time he looks back at her. 'Annie,' she says. 'Our *daughter*. Have you seen her yet?'

'Ah, she met the plane. She didn't tell you?'

'She rang and asked me your flight number. She must have found out somehow. I thought she wanted to stay neutral.'

'Annie? Oh, come on. She's on your side all the way. Never once wavered.'

'Is she?'

'She's *dy*ing to see us back together again.'

'Oh. That's my side? Well, it *was*, of course. Before you turned up in Paris. You and Sandra.'

'I see.' He takes a deep drag of his cigarette, finishes his wine too fast and chokes. He can feel his face reddening. 'Then it's my side she's on.'

'As always. Poor Annie, she's a romantic. So are you, I suppose.'

'I suppose.' He splutters and ducks his head. 'Well, I can do with any help that's going.'

'Thump your back?'

'In a general way, I meant.' He pours more wine.

'We're to live happily ever after, is that the idea?'

'No good?'

'And what about Sandra?'

'All over. Ages ago.'

'Ages?' She is staring into the fire. 'What do you mean, ages? Have you been to her place since you got back?'

'She wasn't there, I just took my things. I think she's going to stay in the States another week or so. She said she might, at the airport. She has a friend she wants to see in Boston.'

'How's her thesis? Finished?'

'Nearly. As far as I know. She was too depressed to work on it much, she said. It has passages of real inspiration.'

'Praise from you, praise indeed. So she saw you off. Is last week *ages* ago?'

'We were under the one roof. Domiciled, is that the word? – under the one roof. Even that was bad enough, after we got back from Paris.'

'Why was that?'

'I told her I'd go home to you. If you'd have me.'

'You didn't tell *me*.'

'She said she'd go whenever I said. She didn't want to go. She wouldn't admit we'd failed. She sat tight and wouldn't be provoked into a quarrel –'

'That's weak.'

'I know. She's a totally passive woman. Dogged and deadpan no matter what you do or say. She won't argue. Won't fight.'

'Weak.'

He nods. 'What I think myself.' Then he catches her eye. 'You're leading me on, aren't you? What am I saying wrong? You're trying to trap me.'

'*You* were weak, that's all. Go on.'

'*I* was? It was a deadlock, we were barely speaking, a disastrous paralysis of the will. I was dying for a show-down and dreading the thought of it. I couldn't throw her out in cold blood, could I? And it dragged on and on.'

'Of course you were sleeping with her.'

'Oh Margie.'

'No right to ask?'

'Of course. Every right.'

He watches her stroke the cat as it winds itself round her ankles. Both of them are dark-haired and glazed by the firelight, their eyes almost shut.

'Well? Were you?' she says.

'Now and then.'

'You *see*.'

'*You* don't. She was just there. That's all it was. It didn't mean a thing to me. Even to her in the end, I think. It was even shocking, how little it had come to mean.'

'You'd say that, of course.'

'No credit for owning up to it?'

'How else could she have stayed? Of course you were sleeping together.'

'I'm trying to tell you what happened. The truth, as a matter of fact.'

'Same old story, isn't it? I hope she's over it by now. More likely she's hoping you'll go back to *her*.'

'All I can say,' and he winces at his own pomposity, 'is that I've never given her the slightest reason for hoping that.'

'What will you do?'

'It seems to be out of my hands now.' This is petulance, when resignation is what he's trying for: angrily he gets up and pours more wine. The bottle has lost its jacket of frost and feels warm, but the wine chills his mouth. She sips and sits staring through the quivering wine in her glass at the flurries and pools the fire makes. He lights a cigarette. 'Not smoking?' he says.

'No.' She grins at him. 'I've given up.'

'More willpower than I've got.' He blows out smoke.

'I should hope so.'

'Isn't that the black dress you bought in Paris?'

'That you bought me in Paris.'

'That you finally let me buy you in Paris.'

'*Enfin* – yes. As it happens.'

'You said you'd never wear it again. When we quar-relled in the Brasserie Lipp. You said it had brought you bad luck.'

'I wonder if Sandra wears hers.' But he doesn't follow. 'Whatever you bought *her*, and don't tell me you didn't.'

'To tell the truth, I did –'

'Of course. To restore parity.'

'I did offer to buy her a dress. I'd let slip about yours and she hadn't said anything but I could sense it was on her mind. She turned it down, though.'

'Silly woman.'

He shrugs. 'She'd rather have books, she said. So I never bought her a thing to wear the whole time we were away.'

'Why the triumphant tone?'

'Why? I did buy her *books*. Lots of old Colettes. There we were in our hotel under our two lamps in a dark little room in the rain, reading Colette and blaming our misery on each other.'

'On each other.' That makes her smile.

'And on ourselves.'

'It never changes anything,' she says wearily. 'Let's not talk about it. I used to think about it all the time. You'd kept me in the dark and I'd never know the whole story. But it's so long since –'

'Not so long, is it? You said –'

'– It's so long since I cared what your life with Sandra was like. Is it just sour grapes? I don't think so.'

He is staring from a face suddenly still and grey.

'Are you sure of that?' he says at last.

'You think I want to hurt you, get my own back, don't you? It's not that. Why meet at all now, if we won't be honest with each other? Don't look like that. What *can* you have been expecting?'

'Not a life sentence.'

'I'm not the judge. I was the victim. That's how *I* felt on the morning you packed and went to live with Sandra. You had sentenced me to despair. I was left wondering how to live through even one day of it.' She stands, rustling her black dress. 'I'll make coffee.'

Clumsily he stands and puts his arms round her, his head in the hollow of her neck. His hair tickles her. 'Coffee already?' he murmurs.

'Please.' She wipes her eyes. 'Listen to me. You haven't been listening.'

'Is there someone else? Is that it?'

'We're at cross purposes, aren't we? There's no one *else*. There's no one.'

'All our years together. Surely –'

'That was what *I* said. Did it make any impression on you?'

'Of course. It did on Sandra too.'

'*You went and told Sandra what I'd said?*'

'Only that. She was always bringing it up. "We've been together for twenty-one days," she'd say, "to your twenty-one years with Margaret." Things like that. Darling, is your hair still black? It looks like honey in the firelight.'

He moves strands of her hair in his freckled hands. It is still black, with here and there a glint of white. Like the cat with raindrops on it, he thinks, and strokes her hair.

'No, don't.' She sits down. 'What did *you* say?'

'Not much I could.'

'She was asking for reassurance, or so it sounds.'

'Reassurance! Exactly.' Sitting, he runs both hands through his own greying ginger hair, a new mannerism of his.

'Why not? You were sure enough before.'

'That was before.'

'She didn't come up to expectations.'

He shakes his head.

'Why did you think *I* would? What do I have to gain by a reconciliation now? Except financially, of course. Obviously we both have a vested interest in staying married.'

'That's not why. At least have the fairness to –'

'*How fair were you?*'

'Okay, sorry. You know very well that money has nothing to do with it, though. Don't you?'

'What has?'

'Love?'

'Security?'

'Love and security, fine. Not financial security.'

'Why, though, would I represent security?' She frowns. 'Unless it's because I represent the past. There's nothing so secure as the past, I suppose. We're like crabs that have had to fight their way out of their old shells. We wish we could crawl back into them. We're afraid the new shells won't harden.'

'*What* new shells?' He pours more wine. 'In a sense you are the past, of course. You're the future as well. The only future that makes sense. At present, I'm stranded.'

'Like me. When I got back from Paris –'

'Oh God. You didn't understand. I *had* to go to Paris –'

'I couldn't face coming straight home. I stopped off in London. I was only away six weeks, but you'd have thought it was six months, to look at the house. Of course it was summer here. But the past! Nothing stays safely the way it was. I'm not the same.'

He says nothing, his gaze on the glowing floor, on the cat nodding, rasping one shoulder with its sharp tongue.

There was such a chilliness, a scum of neglect over everything, she could hardly believe it. Dust sticky on all the glass. The lights blurred and strung with cobwebs. In the bath was a dead baby mouse, stuck there by its black tail, its ears curled and its eyes glinting, its body as light and dry as a moth. In a cupboard potatoes had shrivelled and put out white and purple shoots, two of them long and jointed like feelers. It was as if the house was underwater and in its recesses silent creatures flickered, crabs, lobsters.

'Even the garden,' she says aloud. 'Weeds and slugs,

white spiders in white webs. A crow always grating and swooping, even wasps. Am I imagining this? I thought I might go mad, I was so alone. You were never out of reach before. There were other women, but you lived with *me*, they never lasted. When an affair was over I always knew, you were so sorrowful. Anxious for comfort – reassurance – which you got. And I could comfort myself while you slept with the thought that you were at least *here*, and you couldn't go on betraying me for *ever*. Little enough to look forward to, wouldn't you think? But you're falling harder all the time. You've even left me.'

'Marg. I *was*n't out of reach.'

'Oh! Not out of reach in America? And before that, all the nonsense about your secret hideaway? Not telling a soul her – *your* – address? Ringing me every few hours from public phones to make sure I hadn't slit my *throat*, for God's sake –'

'I know I behaved irrationally –'

'Confessing and then hurtling out with your bags in that *head*long rush –'

'It was the only way I *could* go –'

'Of course people were very kind. Most people just thought you were overseas as planned, on your study leave. The ones who did know said not to worry. He'll be back, dear. It's only the male menopause. Keep his dinner hot. Here's a lovely kitten for you. It'll be company.'

He grimaces. 'I shaved and showered and got dressed in the middle of the second night. I was on the point of coming home. She was so devastated I couldn't do it.'

'She got you to leave *me*. It would have served her right.'

'She did and she didn't. She never had much faith in it. God knows, I soon lost mine. It was as if some other clown in my skin had taken over. While I looked on in horror.'

'That lets you out, then.'

'I know it doesn't. I'm trying to explain.'

'Why didn't she have much faith in it?'

'We hardly knew each other, she said. It was too soon.'

'True enough. Four or five months, wasn't it?'

'I knew I'd lose her if I went to America without her. She'd – she wouldn't stay faithful. And I can't share a woman, you know how I feel about that.'

'Did she say she wouldn't?'

'Virtually.'

'If she was at all honest, she must have known – oh, never mind.' She picks up her glass, but it's empty. He tips the last yellow trickle into the glasses.

'She was honest,' he says doubtfully.

'Up to a point, perhaps.'

'Aren't we all.'

'Oho! You're a special case. So's she, if her honesty can handle sneaking off with married men.'

'She never thought I'd leave you. She knew all along that I was letting infatuation carry me away. She was always saying that.'

'How annoying.'

'Oh, it was.' He gives a short laugh. 'Still, since she was right . . .'

'How smoothly you say it. I was always saying it too.'

'I know it's unforgivable.'

'It would be, for you. We both know that.' It annoys her that he won't look straight at her. 'I always trusted you absolutely not to leave me. That was *my* security.' She picks up the glasses and the bottle, all empty. 'What's the use? It's getting late. Let's have coffee.'

'Late?' He looks amazed.

'I have a class in the morning.'

Lately, she thinks, I've made a ceremony of going to bed. I turn off the lights and break up the embers in the grate. I consign myself carefully to bed, now that I sleep alone. This is late for me.

She leans close to the kitchen window to make its gold reflections vanish when her shadow touches them. A wet moon lies over the shallow garden. Its light is not moving ın the milky puddles: the rain has stopped. She can see scrolls of lilies and a bowed white tree, no taller than she is, its long red branches spilled like hair brushed up from a white nape. The pear tree with its fruits against the white-washed wall. At the top of a column of spines, one many-branched stalk in midair, clustered with pale bells. She steps back. Now the yellow room settles on the glass again. She fills the copper kettle and lights the gas.

He comes out and puts his arms lightly round her from behind. She stands away stiffly, but he pretends not to notice. 'I let the cat out,' he says. 'Okay?'

'Yes.'

'It wanted to go.' She just shrugs. 'Margie?'

'Mmm?'

'*I* don't. Can't I stay?' He presses his face against her hair, patient. 'For old times' sake. Just for tonight.'

'Just for tonight.'

'I'll go quietly in the morning. Anything you say.'

'Tell me the truth: where *are* you staying?'

'At my sister's. At Sheila's. I told you.'

'I'll ask her.'

'Go ahead and ask her.'

'You didn't exactly rush here. What's the rush now?'

'I've walked past here at least ten times in the last four nights.'

'Why's that? Nostalgia?'

'I don't believe I can live without you.'

'Let's talk some other time. I'm tired.'

'What if you get into bed and I bring the coffee in?'

Shrugging, she goes without a word to undress by the slanted light of the lamp by her bed. She brushes her hair, making it swing and crackle in the mirror. She is a pillar of wax, tufted in three places and melting, dwindling, on her arms and shoulders and yellow hips. Look at my hands, she thinks as she pulls back the covers and slips under-neath: like hens' claws. We grow old and none the wiser. She hears him light a match; sigh, as he breathes in smoke.

He makes a deft clatter of spoons and cups. He feels at home now. A cigarette in his demurely smiling mouth, he pads in naked, with one hand holding the coffees and an ashtray and with the other cupping himself shyly.

'*Where* are your clothes?'

'By the fire.'

'*Why*?'

'I'm *freez*ing. Ow. I'll *drop* something.'

'All right. Get in, then. Come on.'

He shakes the bed and the table beside it, spilling the light of the lamp on his back. He looks like a swimmer in sunny water, spotted with light and faded freckles, reaching for the cups once he is in bed. She smells his sweat, like hay, as she remembers, or like wattle flowers, sweet and yeasty, overripe.

The telephone rings in the kitchen.

'I bet that's Sandra.' She crashes her coffee down and drags her bathrobe over her shoulders. 'If it is, she'll be sorry.'

'It won't be,' he says blandly. 'She wouldn't ring here.'

'Anyone's capable of anything, I'm finding.' She hurries out. He smokes quickly, sipping his coffee; he can just hear her murmuring, then a sudden laugh and the bell as she hangs up.

'Annie,' she says, crawling in next to him. 'Being daughterly.'

'Ah.'

'She did at least try to sound surprised that you're here.'

'Ah, well.' He smiles. 'I may have mentioned –'

'So it would seem. At this time of night, too. I've hardly seen her since I got back from Paris, but she's always ringing up. I told her all about it, of course.' She makes a face. '*Joyeux Noel à Paris*, and there you were on the doorstep. With Sandra in tow.'

'My worst Christmas. Three days of hell.'

'When did you know you *had* to go to Paris? You never told me.'

166

'When you wrote that *you* were there. I had to see you. Sandra knew, I suppose. She insisted on coming with me.'

'I wouldn't have told you which hotel if I'd imagined you'd do that.'

'Wouldn't you really?' He has finished his coffee already. She sighs. 'Did you have lots of snow? Back in America?'

'Snow, ice. Everything was white. It wasn't as cold as Paris, though. It never stopped raining, remember?'

'*Il pleut sur la ville —*'

'*Comme il pleure dans mon coeur.*'

'I'll never forgive you, you know. Not as long as I live.'

'No, I know. I'll make it up to you.'

'Not the *temps perdu.*'

'Everything.'

There is a book face-down under the lamp on the table. He peers at the title: Colette's *La Naissance du jour*. She is looking away, so he says nothing. At the edge of the golden light, on the dressing table under the mirror, he notices a deep wooden bowl of persimmons from the tree. The tree itself is outside this window, dripping and moving its tangle of shadows slowly on the blind. 'The Matrimonial Home,' he murmurs reproachfully. She says nothing. He puts his cup down and stubs out his cigarette. 'Peel you a persimmon?' he says.

'No!' she smiles. 'They're too messy to eat in bed. Those aren't even ripe, they're sour. They're for looking at.'

'I'd rather look at you.'

'Don't overdo it, now.'

'Me? When I've missed you so unspeakably?' He takes her empty cup and then lies on his back beside her.

'Turn over,' she says, 'and I'll hold you.' She puts her arm along the curly bulk of his thigh and doesn't speak for so long that he thinks she's asleep, her breath warm on his back. Then he hears her murmur, 'You'll only leave me again.'

'I won't.'

'Don't, please.' And her lips warm on his shoulder.

'Darling, I won't.' He hides his exultation. Turning, he lifts her hair and runs his thumb along the damp white skin of her throat, which is like a lily as the songs say, or like a camelia petal, pale and faintly crazed. Her pulse flickers in it. Two red mounds rise on it like nipples where a mosquito must have bitten her. He licks them. 'Asleep?' he whispers. But she makes a long turn and lies on her back, one arm over him, her eyes in shadow, lightly closed.

All the familiar women with their long white throats and breasts, he thinks. Their soft thighs, where they're warmest, and the rough wet hair between.

With a swish and a rattle of blinds the rain starts again.

'*Il pleut*,' she whispers. 'I can't send you out in this.'

'Good.'

'What were you thinking just now?' Her eyes are open now, dark and wet. He kisses them to close them, then kisses her mouth. 'You were remembering *her*,' she says. 'You can tell me the truth.'

It's not really the truth. 'But Marg, I *was*n't,' he cries out; too despairingly, because he feels her start and recoil. He lights a cigarette. He breathes the smoke in heavily. They move apart in their bed and lie listening to the loud rain.

POMEGRANATES

'YOUR HAIR'S got darker,' Kyria Sophia says, 'since you came here first. Otherwise you're the same. Your Greek is still all right. I can't take it in, how it's all those years since you left our son.'

Strolling around the village on a road that has been asphalted past balconied mansions where doughy cottages used to be, she is slow: she who strode laughing and skipped over its ruts and heaps of dung. She is almost deaf. The skin of her face is baked on, her hair dead white. A grey spider like a crab is groping over threads of it; she stands still to let the younger woman flick the spider off, and absently with ridged hands strokes her woven hair smooth again.

Passing a garden, she begs a bunch of marigolds from a young householder whose moustache just covers a tolerant smile. She grabs at running children to ask each one: whose little boy, whose little girl? Outside the bakery they meet a nephew of hers, a man bald as a brass knob who always makes much of her Australian grandson whenever his father brings him here. Merrily she screws two fistfuls off the loaf he has bought. Munching hot sour bread, talking about their boy, they all walk home in the sun.

In barn after barn left open to air, garlands of tobacco are hanging like fur coats. She and the old man no longer grow any. Their barn still has sacks of grain, bales of hay and lucerne; he keeps the old horse in there, and the cow with her calf. Kyria Sophia has her vegetable garden, fenced with beans and morning glories. Her tomatoes

169

hang in skeins among yellowing leaves. She has round peppers and long ones, deep red, and black eggplants curved like horns. Hens scratch and flounce, and two scraggy turkey cockerels. The flowers on her basil are like lilac, white and mauve.

The trees are the same, in the same warm mist as when Bell first saw them, their leaves yellowed, even the cob-webs afloat among them yellowed. Mist-glossy and black, there are the thorny acacias: dented gold pods, green fronds of leaves. Over the doorway the grapes are ripe to wrinkling and hum all day with insects, grapes so sweet that they parch the throat. Along the fence there are trees with round red fruits too bright to be apples and besides they have tails: pomegranates, full of red glass seeds.

It is seven years since Bell was here last; fourteen, since she first came in pomegranate time.

Kyria Sophia picks one now and breaks it open. She and this Australian who was her daughter-in-law sit on stools under the grapevine, nibbling the seeds.

'The boy kept saying when they came this summer that you had made up your mind to come. I didn't believe it. After all these years. And here you are.'

'I wanted to come before this.'

'I'll pick the pomegranates before you go. You can take some back to Australia for him.'

This is the time of year when the earth reddens, and the sun; and the moon, like an egg in a nest of clouds.

'Every summer they come I tell the boy, this or that is his mother's,' Kyria Sophia says coyly. 'Whenever we use your things.' Forgotten things are everywhere. They have just drunk Nescafe from the silver-rimmed Australian cups, with milk from the old blue-and-white striped jug. Today's yoghurt, in the red French casserole, is warm in an Onkaparinga blanket by the wood stove. Kyria Sophia has the earthenware baking-dish – a wedding present – on her lap: under a white crust is tomato paste, dried like blood after days in the sun. She is spooning off the crust of mould.

'All your things have been waiting here for you.' She sighs when silence answers her.

'What if I go and see if there are any eggs?' Bell jumps up.

'Go and see.'

She escapes to the barn, where the hens lay their eggs in the old mangers. Just inside, the black-lashed eyes of the calf bulge; it stumbles upright, its knees and belly wet with dung. The cow swings her head up from the manger with a snort that stirs the hay warmly. There are four smeared eggs stuck with straw beside the dummy egg.

She remembers the eggs she wrote 'B' on.

'She wrote "B" on the eggs!' Her sister-in-law Chloe's voice. 'Why should she hog them? What about my children?'

'Ssst.' That was the old woman. 'Here she is!'

'So what?'

'Here I am.' She saw Chloe grimace. 'What's wrong?'

'Nothing.'

'Something about eggs?'

'No, no, she didn't say anything.'

'I did.' Chloe pointed. 'That's not fair.'

'Because they're hard-boiled?'

'I'm sure it's just a misunderstanding, girls.'

'How come you need your initials on them?'

'Oh. The "B"? I always – it's for "Boiled". *Brasto*.'

'Oh.'

'So we can tell.'

'There! A simple misunderstanding!'

'I still don't see why you had to hard-boil four, when there aren't any fresh eggs.'

'I thought there would be. I boiled these for the salad.'

'We don't put eggs in the *salad*.'

'No? *Sorry*.'

'They'll do for a *meze* with olives. And Magdalini will have fresh eggs,' smiled Kyria Sophia. 'Let's all go and see her now.'

'Let's go and see Aunt Magdalini?' she is about to call out now, coming back with the eggs. But there is the *papas* fluttering along the road, his coppery hair and beard as if on fire under his black stovepipe hat. 'Look! It's the same *papas*! The seaman, the red one who married us.'

Kyria Sophia's mouth sets hard. 'That's him.'

'He's coming over.'

'He would.'

Both women kiss the red curls of his extended wrist. They all recite the required greetings; then he sinks into the cane armchair with a creak to wait for the cakes and coffee.

Luckily Bell has brought a ribboned box of cakes from the city. She washes her hands and the eggs, pours glasses of water and puts a cake each on three silver-rimmed plates. This *papas*, she remembers, was a wild seaman until his wife made him study theology and give her six boys, burly farmers all. 'I ploughed the waves,' he boomed. 'My boys plough the dry land.' Barbarossa.

'He looks like a pirate!'

But the old woman sniffs, stirring the coffee.

'I ploughed the waves. My boys plough the dry land.' That time, too, he was having coffee with them both. 'Are you still liking Greece, *madame*? Yes? A very different life.'

Bell quoted a proverb: 'Where there's land, there's home.'

'Good, good. Here's the place to raise children.'

'I hope to, father. One day.'

'Soon, if God wills.'

'We'll see.'

'Mmm. How many years is it?' Scratching his bright beard, he leaned forward. 'You do have contact with your husband?'

'Contact? He lives here!'

'No: contact. She doesn't understand!' He rolled his eyes at her mother-in-law, who shot them both a shifty look.

'Contact? Mama, he can't mean –'

'Of course he does!' hissed the old woman.

'Oh.' She felt her red face gape stiffly in a grin. 'Yes. I do.'

'It's the will of God then, eh?' he said gratefully. Both women glared as he took his leave.

'And what's more, your mother put him up to it!' She was still angry when her husband came home. 'What she really wanted him to ask was if I'm on the Pill!'

'Don't start this again,' muttered her husband.

'It's *her*. She never stops.'

'Ssst. Perhaps it was a misunderstanding.'

'Sure.'

'Okay, so she wants grandchildren. What's so terrible about that?'

'Like when she took our dirty clothes –'

'She wanted to help you wash –'

'– to see if some disease was stopping me conceiving!'

'You hurt her that night. Shouting, crying, shutting yourself in.'

'Asking if I'd like to see a doctor! "This stain here on your pants – are you sure nothing's wrong?"'

'Oh God.'

'Oh yes, God, oh yes. "The will of God."'

His curly beard is sprinkled with icing-sugar; he rubs his hands and a veil of it falls. 'Is it the will of God,' he intones now, 'that the churches in your country should have women priests?'

'No!' says the old woman. 'Jesus was born a man. He wasn't born a woman!'

'Mama, He had to be born one or the other.'

'Exactly! And He chose to be born a man. He said woman was born to be man's hostage!'

'What? Hostage!'

'He said so in the Bible. And now the Protestants have women priests! Blasphemers! God will send His fire to Earth!'

'Because of that?'

'The world will end soon in storms of fire. That's the nuclear holocaust. No wonder, when mankind has forsaken His way and let communism and divorce and women's liberation run wild. They worship the Antichrist! May God send the fire to burn them!'

'Well now, Kyria Sophia, time I was on my way.' The *papas* sighs. 'Duty calls. Have you got the names?'

'I'll bring them, father.'

Tomorrow is Psychosavvato, Souls' Saturday, when he will hold a morning service for the souls of everyone's dead. Their names will be read out, and each family's *kollyva* shared among the mourners. Kyria Sophia will be the first one there.

After the afternoon sleep they go to see Aunt Magdalini, who insists on picking all her best roses and presenting them with a hug of welcome. She scuttles in the blue cave of her kitchen dishing out cherry *glyko* on glass saucers, mixing coffee, pouring iced water.

'*Aman*, Magdalini.' Kyria Sophia slaps her saucer down. 'This cherry *glyko* of yours. Nobody can eat it. Throw it away.'

'I boiled it too long,' cackles Magdalini.

'Is it *glyko* or glue?'

'Don't eat it, dear, if you don't like it,' Magdalini tells the visitor.

'Oh, but it's lovely!' she answers. It's more like toffee than jam. She scoops up the last threads and bites them off her spoon, grinning at Magdalini, who is more than ever a gnome of a little old woman. Kyria Sophia hunches her shoulders and her black brows. Magdalini, as ever, is impervious.

'I haven't boiled my *kollyva*,' she says. 'Have you?'

'Oh yes,' says Kyria Sophia.

'I haven't even cleaned the wheat.'

'Bring it here, then.'

Magdalini brings in a pan of rustling wheat. The three women sweep it with their hands, picking out stones and husks and seeds. The mist hovering in the doorway turns cool blue.

Kyria Sophia has a bowl of *kollyva* with a lighted candle stuck in it, as if for a birthday; and a little brass incense holder which she stuffs with hot coals from the *somba* before setting in it a bead of red incense like a pomegranate seed. She takes them from room to room. The smoke trails after her muttering shadow.

Back in the kitchen, sighing, she strains the evening milk and puts it on to boil.

The old man comes in cold from the *kafeneion*, hungry for chestnuts before dinner. He smokes with his eyes closed, waiting. Kyria Sophia has to remind Bell where to find the chestnuts. She remembers without being told how to slit them with a knife and shuffle them round on the iron top of the *somba* until they scorch. Singeing her fingers, she peels them then, enough for everyone; waxen, wrinkled and sweet, they sting in the mouth.

Kyria Sophia cuts bread and cheese and heats up the vegetable stew left over from lunch. The old pots flutter their lids and whistle, now and then uttering a faint crow as of roosters in the distance. The milk, as always, boils over, surrounding the pot with a frill that crackles and burns brown. They eat eggplants and peppers and beans and mop up all the red oil with their bread. The cheese is a salty white honeycomb, the grapes ripening into raisins. To celebrate her coming, they pour what's left of last year's ouzo from the demijohn, and drink it watered.

While Bell washes up, Kyria Sophia decides to inspect the eggbound hen. 'I hope she's managed to lay it. If not –' She hólds up the knife. 'I'm not letting her die on me.' Soon squawks and one screech come from the henhouse. A bundle thumps on the kitchen windowsill by the pot of basil: red cords poke from speckled shoulder feathers. Kyria Sophia throws open the window – oil-yellow smoke drifts out among needles of rain – and with a pot of boiling water at her elbow she plucks and cleans the hen.

'Rain at last. Well, we'll eat her tomorrow.' She crams the carcase into the refrigerator. (They have one now, and a television set too.) 'In red sauce? Or egg-and-lemon, maybe.' Her bloody fingers hold up a bright pomegranate: no – the egg that she pulled out. 'Pity,' she says.

She sits by the *somba* reading the prayer book aloud in her cracked treble, glancing over her glasses now and then. The visitor goes and leans over the sill to breathe in the cold air made lemony by the wet basil. In the mud below, the cat's eyes flash green; it sends up a yowl for more of the tattered hen. Both the old people are snoring.

So many village evenings spent yawning beside the *somba*, to the sounds of cats and snores and night birds. She has put off going to bed, because this is the same old bedroom, and the bed. Those are the two cane armchairs that made up a cot for the baby the first time he was here. These are even the honeymoon sheets that they rumpled and soaked with sweat all the first summer, night and afternoon. Now she opens the window and the hinged shutters: she leans on the sill. The rain has stopped. Drops fall from the grapes into dark puddles.

On the chest by the bed are old photographs of them all together, here and in the city and on beaches. She is holding one of her boy tossing wheat to hens long since killed and eaten, when his grandmother creeps in.

'Some hot milk?'

'No thanks, Mama.'

'All the good times.' She points at the photograph. 'Don't they matter any more?'

'Everything matters.'

'Can a woman just walk out on her man these days, and her little boy? Don't you remember how it was?'

'I remember, or why would I be here?'

'I can't take it in.' She turns away. 'Hang anything you want in this wardrobe. See, we have a wardrobe now. I'll just take my coat for church, then I won't have to wake you tomorrow.' Her voice is still reproachful. Once she would have added: Or will you come with me? She holds up a slim camelhair coat, silk-lined. 'Isn't it beautiful?'

'Yes. Let me see it on.'

She slips it on and lets her white plait loose.

'Yes, Mama, you look very elegant.'

'I'm old.' Peering in the dull wardrobe mirror: 'Look at me. Is my hair much whiter now? Whiter than when you first saw me? It must be.' There are tears on her cheeks.

'No.' Bell puts her arms round her. 'It's the same.'

OUR LADY OF THE BEEHIVES

1

Barbara, in the dark beside Andoni, felt swollen all over, raw and gritty from the day's sun and salt and sand. Like a hard-boiled egg her body held the heat in. She had dreamt again that some great whining insect, a bee or a wasp, had stung her. In this dream she was asleep on the beach in the noon sun. Waking as the sting pierced her, she was alarmed to see darkness. The harsh slow sound she heard was not waves, but Andoni's breathing.

Vassilaki cried out in his sleep. She got up and knelt with her cheek against his. 'Mama?' he murmured.

'*Nani*,' she said. 'Go to sleep.' But he was fast asleep.

She sighed. It was too hot to lie awake. Instead she crept into the shadows of the sittingroom, switched on the hard light and tore two pages out of her diary to write a letter to her sister.

Dear Jill (she would address it Poste Restante),
I hope you arrived safely and love Athens. We're all fine here. It was great to see you and Marcus. We've just moved into a better house, the Captain's, no less, two floors furnished. The bedrooms are upstairs, with homespun sheets and lots of chairs, a table, but the roon · are large and full of heat – bare planks for floors. Downstairs we cook and eat and keep cool. We have a marble-slabbed bench with a sink and a tap –

*running water! — and a portable gas stovetop with two large
burners and a little one for the coffee* briki. *(If we run out of gas
a neighbour's child will run to the* kafeneion *for us and along
will come the* kafedjis *with a new bottle on his motor scooter.)
The Captain and family have moved next door. His wife has
left us plates, cups, glasses, cutlery, pots, pans, baskets . . .
There's a large round dining table, painted shiny green, and
ten rush-bottomed chairs. There are spiky bundles of herbs —
mostly* rigani *— hung like birch brooms on the wall, and plaits
of onions and garlic, and shrivelled hot red peppers on a string:
we are to help ourselves. Her yellow tabby sits on guard day
and night.*

And as if all that were not enough, this house has a lid!

*Well, it has an indoor staircase, as well as the usual cement
outside one: an indoor ladder, really, fixed into the floor and
leading to a trapdoor set in the planks above. The* kapaki, *they
call it: the lid. The older houses all have one. It props open on
its hinges, or there's a ring in the wall to hook it into, or you can
keep it shut — the sensible thing, Andoni's mother says, when
there's a child to worry about. The lid looks too heavy for
Vassilaki, but it's not, only awkward to lift. Besides, any one
of us, being unused to houses with lids, might step into space
where floor should be. (She looks on the dark side.) So we
don't let Vassilaki go near it. (The Captain's wife agrees.)*

It's like Treasure Island!

*For the rest: no bath, but as the Captain said, with the sea so
near who needs one in summer? And in an annexe behind the
kitchen there's a cubicle with a sit-down toilet, a sewered one, a
bucket of water to flush it, and a plastic waste-paper basket for
the used paper which we mustn't ever flush, only burn.*

*As for the washing, we heat water in a sooty pan of the
Kapetanissa's, kindling a fire under it in the yard with twigs
and brambles, wads of newspaper and (yes) used toilet paper.
We wash the clothes in plastic basins and rinse them in the
wheelbarrow with the hose . . . In short, it's bliss!*

*I wish you could come and see, but of course you have to get
back to London. Tell Marcus the whole town asks after him*

('that brother of yours, is it, that Marko') and please write soon.

Much love,
Barbara.

It was not what she had meant to write, but it would have to do. In the yellow glare she flicked over the pages she had written when Vassilaki was a baby. A couple of pages, that was all, in two years. She was always tired.

> *He lies in my arms* (she read).
> *To sleep he has to suck one fist and clamp the other in my hair, or in his own.*
> *When he cries and I pick him up he sobs, pushing his face into my armpit, like our old cat.*
> *I unwrap his heavy napkin. He has a small pink bag, seamed and ruched, and above it a pink stalk that extends itself and squirts, like some sea creature.*
> *With a grunt he squeezes out mustard, soft lobster mustard.*
> *He presses on the white bags that give him milk, and opens and shuts his vague eyes.*

It might be a girl this time, she thought. We can call her Eirini and that will gratify Andoni's mother. Andoni would have to be told soon, when the time was right. It was a wonder he hadn't guessed. He had something on his mind.

When she sank back on the bed in the dark, Andoni took her in his arms and drove fiercely inside her. Neither of them spoke. He was slippery all over. He hissed like a dolphin surfacing, and then subsided. They drifted back into sleep.

Tomorrow, thought Kyria Eirini, waking as the house sighed and crackled in the dark, tomorrow I'll go to the church. To the Panagia of the Beehives. For Varvara's sake.

The Panagia *sta Melissia*, as it is known, was hardly a church at all, compared to the proper one in the town square, Agios Nikolaos, the patron saint of sailors. The Panagia's was little more than a *parekklesi*, a chapel built to honour a promise by the grandfather of the man who kept the bees now. If the Panagia would save his sons in the storm that had wrecked the fishing boats – he stood watching from the hill among the torn acacia trees – he would build Her a chapel, he vowed. He built it in the shape of a bee box, but with a small square tower, and mixed blue in the whitewash to make it the same colour as the hives. The oil lamp before the ikon of the Panagia would never go out, the old mothers of the town made sure of that.

Inside there was a rustling, never pure silence, even when no one was there; and when the lamps were lit for a *litourgeia* an amber light filled it. The candles on sale at the entrance were made of the pale beeswax, and smelled of honey as they burned. An itinerant artist, having covered the walls and ceiling with images of haloed saints, had painted the shawled Panagia Herself with a gilded Child in skirts, in a garden full of lilies and large brown bees.

Kyria Eirini, turning over on her bed in the hot house, told herself to go and light a candle to the Panagia in the morning. Two candles: one for her dead Vassili, whose sins were forgiven; and one to ask Her to do something. And this morning I won't wake Andoni to go and buy fish, I'll let him off. I'll make *imam bayildi* for lunch instead, she thought; and fell asleep again.

The Captain's daughter, Voula, lying awake in her room next door, saw the gold lozenge of their sittingroom light fall on the balcony, and later disappear. It was Andoni, she thought. 'I love you, Voula, my darling,' she whispered in English, though she had only ever heard Andoni speak Greek. She saw herself on the balcony again, brushing out her hair in swathes, hair smelling of rain water; and Andoni looking on. How could such a man have married a thin ginger-yellow oblivious foreign broomstick of a woman like Barbara?

It was almost as if he were not married at all.

She stood up. Her mother was snoring in the next room. She crept out of the cracking house, past other moon-white houses and along a dusty path fenced with sharp thistles to a beach out of sight of the town. The lights of the grigri boats were as small as the stars. She dropped her clothes on the dry sand and padded across the black suede of the wet sand with its cold pools of stars, knotting her hair in a crown as she went, to keep it dry. Then she ran straight into the thick water. The shock of it made her shudder. It was so cold it was as if she had been cut in half: she could neither feel nor see herself below the waist. She bobbed down and quickly up. Her breasts glowed, dropping glints of water. Her feet stung now where thistles had scratched them. Blood pounded in her head.

If she floated, her face lying on the water would be a mirror of the moon. But then she would wet her hair. She would be found out. A moon afloat in black ice.

The heroine of a book she had read swam alone at night. She was a sea-girl too, a fisherman's daughter, the foundling child of a mermaid; and a man watched her, watched Smaragdi in the water. But that was not why, Voula insisted to herself: I love swimming at night and I always have and I always will.

But she knew that this time she was hoping that Andoni, unable to sleep, would sense where she was and follow her.

'Who's there?' she would say, splashing to make a surface of froth to cover her.

'Andoni,' he would say. 'Did I frighten you?'

What would she say? 'No. It's all right.'

'What?' he would falter. He would not be sure.

'A little. But don't go. It's all right.' She moved her cold hands over her breasts. His hands would be dry, warm.

A whimper came from the shore. She stiffened, horrified. On the grey sand a shadow was moving towards her clothes. With a gasp she sank to her nose to hide. She could see a white body, long-legged, white-scarved: no, it was a goat. 'Meh,' it said.

With a snort of alarmed laughter Voula splashed out. '*Fige,*' she hissed, and it stared at her. '*Fige!*' She slapped its burry rump and it trotted off, its frayed rope hopping behind it. Glancing anxiously at shadows, she dragged her clothes on to her wet skin and hurried along the path. Thistles slashed her. The goat, looking back, leaped and was gone. Moonlight lay heavy and white on shuttered walls. Nothing moved. Her shadow was sharp, and at every streetlamp a dim one joined it, grew and dwindled away. It reminded her of the game she played with Vassilaki's shadow when they went to the beach; Andoni's little boy. Her step was light as the shadows falling. No one seeing her out at this time of night would doubt why.

The door creaked, but her mother snored on. She laid herself cool and dry on her bed, and yawned. Bubbles of blood stung on her ankles. The moon was blue stripes on a wall.

A loud door creaked, waking Barbara, but no other sound followed. The house creaked a lot as the night cooled. She lay and thought that the air in the room was like coal in a fire, black and steadily smouldering. It would be good to walk through the grey dust of the streets now. The boats would be converging out at sea, gathering in the net. *Savridia*, she thought; *kefalopoula, marides, barbounia, fagri, sardelles*. She knew more fish in Greek than in English. It would be good to wade into cold black water flickering with fish. But there would be a scandal if anyone saw her. Besides, she was tired.

With a sigh she turned her soaked body over. A donkey sobbed, a goat gave a sudden meh–eh–eh. Soon the roosters would wake. Soon Andoni's mother would knock on the door and call Andoni to go and buy fish, unless she slept in. Soon Vassilaki would wake, waking them all.

She closed her eyes and slept.

2

Voula met Andoni coming out of the water with his speargun and flippers, pushing his mask up on to his rough hair. 'Hullo, did you catch any?' she said.

'No. None there.'

'Bad luck.'

'You're looking very beautiful today.'

'I look very beautiful every day.'

'Is that so?'

She only smiled and swung away, ruffling the surface. That he was watching her made her aware of all her colours and shapes intensified in the morning sea. In a few minutes he waded back in and floated and swam lazily some metres away. But neither of them spoke again.

This morning as usual Barbara had clothes and napkins to wash, soaking in a basin on the back *taratsa*. She wrung them out and with a grunt hurled the dirty water into the vegetable garden. Hens skittered. She poured powder and hot clean water on the clothes and pumped and kneaded them. There were ripe grapes already in the vine above her head, and flies crowded in them. The morning sun shone through grapes and leaves; she looked on the ground for green reflections, as if they were made of glass; but the shadows were black. They were sharp in the still light. Strange, thought Barbara, brushing sweat off her eyebrows, how shadows look sharper on a still day, as if a wind would blur air as it blurs water. Bubbles catching the sun in her basins of clothes were like white opals.

Kyria Eirini swept the leaves and hens' droppings off the

dry earth of the yard with a straw broom with no handle, then rinsed and wrung out the clothes with Barbara and helped her hang them out. Then she went in to tidy up. When she opened the shutters and panes to air the rooms, the sun fell in thickly and whatever was inside glowed, furred with gold. No matter how often she dusted, more dust drifted in and settled. At least it's fresh dust, thought Kyria Eirini. Insects buzzed in and out.

She was glad when Barbara and Vassilaki went to the beach at last, to the same spot as always, so she knew where to find them. She would rather stay and be alone in the Kapetanissa's kitchen. She boiled rice in milk and honey to make *rizogalo*, stirred it and poured it on to plates to cool before she tapped cinnamon over its tightening lumpy skin. Andoni and Vassilaki loved her *rizogalo*. She sliced doughy eggplants and salted them, sliced onions and garlic and tomatoes. She breathed in the smell as the olive oil smoked in her hot pans. 'God be praised,' she muttered. 'Everything we need, He gives us.' She slid slices of egg-plant in and the oil frothed over them.

Barbara came to life only in the sea. Her speckled body glowed, magnified, and made its green gestures metres above her shadow on the sea floor. Pebbles were suddenly large then small as the water moved. She dived to grasp one. A bird must feel like this, she thought as she dived and twisted, gasped, the bubbles pounding in her ears: a bird flying in rain. When she came up a white net of light enfolded her lazily.

When she came out of the water she lay on a towel with another towel over her back to keep off the sun. Dazed, she watched the sea. Whenever she blinked she saw a flare of red; then the green sea, then the red flare again, as regular as a lighthouse lamp.

Kyria Eirini bent over her eggplants arranged like small black boats in the pan, ladling the filling of onions and tomatoes more carefully than usual into each one: the pan would be on show in the baker's oven. Barbara would be annoyed with her for struggling down the hot road to the bakery with it, when they could have had something easy for lunch. The thought of Barbara's annoyance was almost as pleasant as the thought of how Andoni would carry the pan home, sucking his fingers coppery with oil when he arrived because he had picked at it on the way.

So she struggled, hot in her black clothes, down the road to the baker's, exchanging greetings as she went. She pointed out to the baker exactly where she wanted her pan, and he told her that he knew his oven as he knew his own hand. She bought a hot white loaf and went on to the Melissia to light a candle to the Panagia, which was after all the real reason she was there.

The church was stuffy and dim, with a rosemary smell of old burnt incense. The glazed faces of the saints stared. Kyria Eirini crossed herself and slipped her drachmas into the box for two candles. One she stuck in the tray of sand, for the dead; one in the iron bracket, for the living. The Panagia held her dwarfish Christ to one blue shoulder, her hollow eyes stern.

'It's not for myself,' she thought to the ikon. 'It's for my daughter-in-law. The Australian one. Fool though she is. *Aman*. Has she no pride? Enlighten her, help her, I pray. And the girl too, save her from temptation. Andoni is turning out just like his father was, whose sins are forgiven.'

As she was leaving, a bee settled on her sleeve. She shook it off. It hovered. 'Xout!' she said. They blundered together out into the sunlight.

At home she wrapped the bread in a cloth. Her dress was stuck to her. She swilled cold water from a bucket over the speckled kitchen floor to wash it. Its stones came to life, all their colours, like shingle on a sea floor. The cat that came with the house, and spent the mornings dozing under the table, sprang up on a chair and spat at her. 'Xout!' spat Kyria Eirini. The cat fled to the window sill and hunched there with a brazen scowl.

When Andoni walked in, Kyria Eirini was scrubbing spots out of the washing before Barbara got home. She started and looked guilty. 'You're home early,' she said.

'I said I'd buy the bread.'

'I bought it.'

'Why? When I told you I'd go!'

'I wanted to light a candle. It was on my way. I took a pan of *imam bayildi* as well. You can get that if you like.'

'*Aman*, Mama! You could just as easily cook it here.'

'Yes, but you like it better baked.'

'Not when it's so much more work.'

'But since it's better?'

'Tiring yourself out for nothing. It's madness.'

Andoni's reaction was all she could have hoped.

'Kyria Eirini?' came Voula's voice at the gate. Still in her bathing suit, she was hugging a pile of striped *kilimia*. 'We thought – my mother and I thought – do you need more blankets at night?'

'Ach.' Flustered, Kyria Eirini waved her soapy hands. 'Thank you. That's very kind.'

'I'll leave them upstairs, will I?'

'Yes, there's a good girl. Thank you.'

Voula, padding into the dark kitchen, ran into Andoni before she saw him, he was so dark himself.

'Careful.' He climbed up ahead to hold the *kapaki* open.

Voula laughed. 'I grew up in this house.'

'All the same.'

'My father fell through once. He was drunk at the time.'

'Didn't you ever fall through?'

'I wasn't allowed to go near it.'

'So you never did?' He followed her and shut the trapdoor.

'No, I was a good girl.'

'Was. And now you're not.'

'Is that what you think, is it?'

'I'm hoping to find out. How old are you?'

She blushed. 'Old enough.' No, this was going too far: she looked round for something safe to remark on, and saw waxy lilies in a vase of her mother's. 'Pretty,' she said.

'Take one.' He lifted one out, its curled stalk dripping.

'Oh, no.' She stepped back. 'Are they from Kyria Magda?'

'Why not? Some old woman with whiskers gave them to your mother. Her goat got out and ate half your mother's beans last night, haven't you heard? You will. You're getting a bucket of milk too. Your mother hates them, she says, so here they are.' He nodded the lily at her. 'Take it, come on.'

'They make her sneeze,' she explained.

'Too big to wear.' He held it up to her hair. 'Pity.'

'How can I take it? It would look – I can't.'

With a stare he dropped the lily out the window. Shocked, Voula ran into the sittingroom with the *kilimia*. He climbed back down to wait, letting the *kapaki* slam shut. But Voula left the house, trembling, by the outside stairs.

Andoni trudged off to the bakery.

3

It was a relief when lunch was over. Barbara and Andoni assured Kyria Eirini that the *imam bayildi* was delicious. But the baker had burnt one edge of it, and besides she thought there was just a little too much salt. They didn't think so. Vassilaki refused to eat any and filled up on all the *rizogalo*.

The washing was dry by then, hooked on the barbed wire fence among the speckled pods, green and red, of the Kapetanissa's climbing beans. Drops of water, falling from their bathers, rolled and were coated with dust. A shirt and a napkin had fallen on to the red earth. They would have to be washed all over again. Barbara sighed. Nothing seemed to dry without its earth or rust or bird stain.

The Kapetanissa had green onions and garlic growing as well as beans, and eggplants with leaves like torn felt, and cucumbers, potatoes, tomatoes, wilting melon vines. Her hens and the rooster had squeezed through the wire and were scratching and jabbing among the watered roots. Brown papery birds, murmuring to themselves, their eyes half-closed. Weary of summer.

Vassilaki had seen them too. He ran in by the gate to chase them out, but they pranced loudly into hiding. 'Xout!' he shouted.

'Vassilaki?' She had folded the clothes and was up to the napkins now. 'Where are you?' He came padding out. She pulled the wire over the gatepost. He was holding a long funnel-shaped pale flower.

'*Kitta*, mama,' he said. 'Look.' His mother had different words for everything.

'Mm. It's a lily. Where was it?' she said. Then: 'Put it down quick. Quick! There's a bee in it.'

So there was, when he looked. A bee with brown fur was crouched, its legs twitching, in the buttery glow at the bottom of his lily.

'Why?'

'It wants that yellow dust, see? On those little horns? It wants to make honey. *Meli*. Put it down now.'

'Why?'

'It might bite.'

'Why?' He held it out at arm's length.

'It might think you want to hurt it.'

'Nao,' he told it.

'Just put it down.'

'*Echo melissa*,' he called over the fence to the Kapetanissa and Voula, who had come out to see why the hens were squawking, and were packing the earth back round the roots with their sandalled feet.

'Careful, she bite you!' Voula called back, but softly in case she woke the neighbours.

'*Ela*, Voula!'

'Put it *down*, Vassilaki!'

He dropped his lily. The bee flew out, made a faltering circle and then was lost among the oleanders.

'*Paei*,' he sighed.

'Yes. It's gone.'

'*Paei spiti?*'

'Yes, it's gone home.'

'*Pounto spiti?*'

'In a bee box. On the hill near the church.' He looked puzzled. '*Konta stin ekklesia*.'

'Why?'

'*Paei na kanei meli*,' smiled Voula, shading her eyes. She followed her mother inside.

'Mama?'

'Yes. It's gone to make honey.'

'*Einai kakia*.'

'Who's bad? Voula?'

'Bee.'

'No, it's not, it's good – *kali*. But you have to leave it alone. You can pick up the lily now it's gone.'

'*Nao*.' They left it lying there.

He went ahead of her up the outside stairs – the wall was too hot to touch – and through the empty sittingroom behind the balcony. He had gone when she came up with the washing. '*Pou eisai?*' she whispered. 'Keep away from the *kapaki*.' When there was no answer she looked in the bedroom: only Andoni, asleep. She found Vassilaki in the next room, on his back on the bed beside the black heap that was his grandmother. His eyelids fluttered as she kissed his cheek; he brushed the kiss away with a loose hand. His hair was damp. '*Nani*,' she whispered. He was already asleep. The room burned with a buttery glow like that inside the lily.

The floor creaked as she crept in, her soles rasped the planks, but Andoni stayed asleep, as if stunned, his mouth open. He had thrown the sheet off. He glistened, brown all over and shadowed with black hairs, barred as well with shadows that fell from the window over him. She lay down beside him in her dress: they would all be getting up soon. The rough cotton was stuck to her. Her breasts ached. Andoni muttered something indistinct. She sighed, hearing a mosquito whine. Our four bodies in the house, she thought, four bubbles of blood, and a fifth still forming, afloat on our white beds. A hollow light seeped through the shutters. Time and the sun stood still.

4

When they awoke, the women always brought coffee and glasses of water up to the balcony. Andoni read the newspapers there. The shadows grew longer almost as they watched, until the street was filled with them. Sometimes a sea breeze rose: the *batis*. Ach, *o batis*, people would say to each other with relief. Sometimes – especially when there was no sea breeze – the family went back to the beach for a late swim, in water warmer and brighter, tawny-shadowed and full of reflections different from its morning ones. Then the sun shrank, spilling its last light along the hoods of the waves.

This afternoon there was no sea breeze.

'Will you drink a little coffee?' And Barbara woke with a start. Kyria Eirini's grey head was at the door. 'Sorry, Varvara. Were you asleep? Vassilaki's awake.'

'Oh, not just yet, Mama, thank you.'

'Well, whenever you like.' She closed the door. Barbara lay blinking in the hot stillness. There was a crushed hollow beside her; she had not heard Andoni go. Her wrists and ankles itched and had red lumps all over them.

She found a mosquito on the dim wall, slapped it, and was trying to wipe off the red smear with spit when the door opened again.

'Varvara, sorry. Vassilaki wants to go to the beach. Ach, not a mosquito? I sprayed too.'

'One. Look at me.'

'It's your sweet blood, you see. Vassilaki is insisting. Can you see any more?' They both peered up. 'No, it was just that one, Varvara *mou*.'

Vassilaki was insisting. '*Thalassa, thalassa, thalassa*,' he chanted.

'We were there all morning,' Bàrbara moaned.

'*Thalassa pame*, Mama!'

'Mama *nani*,' reproached his grandmother, stopping him in the doorway.

'Let his father take him,' Barbara said.

'He go to buy newspaper,' came Voula's voice in English. 'I take him, if you like.'

'Voula, would you? Come in.'

Voula came to the doorway, a coffee cup in her hand, with the other hand gathering her hair at her nape then letting it flow free. Vassilaki pushed past her: 'Mama!' Kyria Eirini made an apologetic face at Barbara and plucked at his shirt. '*Mi*, Yiayia!' And he shook her hand off.

'Come with me today?' Voula squatted beside him.

'*Pou?*'

'*Sti thalassa?*'

'Mama?'

'Mama *nani*.'

He faltered, scowling, but finally took her hand. They went downstairs to the shadowed garden to get a towel from the wire fence and find his bucket and spade. Then they came hand in hand out into the yellow evening. When he started to drag his feet, Voula dodged to make her shadow cover his, and he laughed, remembering how she always played the shadow game; and she remembered the moonlit streetlamps. 'What! You have no shadow!' she said.

'I have so!' He made his shadow escape and caper ahead.

'You have not!' Hers pounced on it again. 'You see? Where it is?'

'There!'

Families sitting on balconies looked on smiling.

Going past Kyria Magda's Voula saw from the corner of her eye that the ivory-necked lilies had gone from the pots on the *taratsa*. The white goat, tied to a post, fixed its slit brass eyes on Voula and said, 'Meh-eh.'

'Meh-eh. Meh-eh,' said Vassilaki. '*Alogaki?*' If it was a horse, then he could ride it.

'*Katsika einai,*' explained Voula, not knowing the English word. '*Echei gala.*'

'*Pou?*'

She pointed to the pink bag bouncing between the stiff hind legs; Vassilaki stooped to look, and giggled. Kyria Magda, screeching hullo, staggered across the yard with a bucket of water. 'All right then, drink, you little whore': and the goat, in its thirst, plunged its chin and ears deep, and sneezed, rearing. 'Run away, will you?' said Kyria Magda, her hands on her hips. 'I'll teach you. Yes, I'll teach her,' she told the watchers; a sour smile crossed her face.

'*Kakia yiayia,*' said Vassilaki when they were well past.

All the way to the beach Voula let him keep ahead of her with his shadow, making little rushes forward whenever he flagged, so that they arrived sweaty and out of breath. She dipped herself in the water, no more, not wanting to take her eyes off him for a moment; though he always paddled in the shallows and if he did stray further out there was a sandbank. Waistdeep, he was filling his bucket with water and spilling it on his head. It splashed all round him and sent ripples flickering up. From his hair, darker and flatter now, bright drops went on falling.

'Ooh! *Kitta*, Voula!'

She sprang to her feet. '*Ti?*'

'*Kitta! Psarakia!*'

'*Pou?*'

'*Na!*' He pointed. There were the little fish, when she looked, first like silver needles, then like black ones. He sank his bucket in bubbles to the bottom to catch them. She lay down again, resting on her elbows. In the distance the boats were tied to the pier. A small one was pulled up on the sand nearby with an octopus spread to dry over its lamps, swarming with wasps. No one else had come down to the beach. I am beautiful, Voula decided; but he's not here to see. Over the sandbank the water was a honeycomb, a golden net. Vassilaki was intent. Now with his bucket, now with his spread hands, he bent to catch fish. '*Psarakia?*' he pleaded. '*Psarakia?*'

They stayed until the sun turned the long shoals red.

Andoni, hunched over a newspaper, saw them coming home along the street, its dark patches not only shadow now but wet dust where the shopkeepers had hosed it. At the other end of the balcony his mother and the Kapetanissa sat making lace with crochet hooks, each of them ignoring her own quick fingers to covertly watch the other's.

'When it's wet it smells like coffee,' remarked Kyria Eirini. 'The earth, I mean.'

'Here comes Vassilaki,' said Andoni.

'Ach, good!' She swung round. 'Yes, here they are!' Sounding too relieved, she knew: the Kapetanissa bridled. Did they think the child might not have been safe with her Voula, did they? She raised her heavy brows.

'Are they late, perhaps?'

'No! Not at all!' They were laughing, licking icecreams. 'Look, she bought icecreams.' Kyria Eirini made her voice soothing. 'She gets on so well with him, doesn't she?'

The Kapetanissa was not satisfied. Andoni picked a

sprig of basil from the nearest pot, rubbed it and sniffed at the green mash his fingers made. His mother waved to Voula and Vassilaki, who waved back.

'I noticed yesterday what a beautiful swimmer she is,' Kyria Eirini went on, making it clear that of course he had been in good hands. 'May we not cast the Evil Eye on her,' she added, as custom demanded after praise, and pretended to spit. The Kapetanissa smiled at her, appeased.

'Yes, she's a genuine mermaid. Everyone says so.'

'Who's a mermaid?' Barbara called lazily from inside, having caught the one word *gorgona*.

'Voula. They're home,' answered Andoni's mother.

'Oh, good.' Barbara went on reading. She knew she was a better swimmer than Voula any day.

Vassilaki's chest had pink trickles on it where icecream had dripped through the soggy tip of the cone faster than he could suck it. Voula flapped the towel – it had lumps of wet sand on it – and hung it on the fence. 'Have a wash?' she said, and pulled the slack hose through from the garden. Vassilaki loved the first wash, the sun-warmed water in the hose. He pulled his shorts open and squeezed his eyes shut waiting for the silver water to come coiling over him. When it did he gave a yell. Voula stooped down to swill the sand and the icecream off him. But the water was running cold now and he squirmed away, giggling as if it tickled.

'Come here.' She was giggling too.

'Nao!'

'There is sand on you!'

'Nao!'

Neither of them had heard any buzzing or seen a wasp or a bee hanging, its wings rippling the air. But now Voula felt a searing stab in her thigh. She screamed with pain and shock.

'*Ti?*' shrieked Vassilaki.

Voula was slapping at her thigh, staring round wildly. Whatever it was fell twitching in a puddle. She bent over it:

196

impossible to tell now if it was a wasp or a bee. She crushed it with her hard heel.

'*Melissa!*' Vassilaki shrieked again. He peered at the crushed shell. Was it his bee? Would it dart up and sting him next? A hen jabbed and took it, spraying mud on him as she skipped away. '*Paei!*' yelled Vassilaki. '*Voula mou!*'

But this was not his Voula, cupping her stung thigh, her face red and twisted. Vassilaki stared. This was not his Voula. He stumbled into the kitchen. No one. 'Mama *mou!* Mama!' He bolted up the wooden steps and raised the trapdoor.

'Vassilaki!' screamed his mother's voice. He swung around in bewilderment – where was she? – and the trapdoor fell shut with a thud above him, jamming his fingers. He screamed loudly, lost his balance and tumbled down the steps on to the floor.

5

At first everyone had thought that the screams they heard were part of the game with the garden hose. Now they all came running. Barbara scrambled through the trapdoor and down the steps to pick Vassilaki up. She sat on the cold floor of the kitchen holding him against her. For long moments he held his mouth open in a silent roar, turning dark red. Then at last sobs and tears burst out. 'Oh, oh, oh,' moaned Barbara in the Greek way that always soothed him best, rocking with each 'oh'.

'*Ponaei!*' he wailed.

'Oh, oh, *poulaki mou,*' she murmured helplessly.

Andoni crouched over him and ran his hands over the wet quivering little body, the yellow mat of hair. There was a lump there and blood seeping; grey splinters showed in the plump flesh of his arms and legs; but no bones were broken. Red tangles were printed on Barbara's dress where he had laid his head.

'What happened?' said Andoni.

'The *kapaki*. He fell downstairs.'

'I know that.'

'*Ponaei!*' Vassilaki touched his head and shrieked when he saw blood on his hands.

'Oh, don't cry, no, no. It'll be better soon.' She kissed his hair.

'*Melissa*, Mama,' he snuffled.

They looked, but there was no sign of a bee sting.

'*Ma pou, poulaki mou?*'

'*Ti* Voula.' He pointed.

Voula, her face swollen with crying and as red as his, was standing in her bathing suit at the kitchen doorway. 'A *melissa* bite me and he frighten,' she said. 'And he hurt his self. The *kapaki* fall on him.' Her thigh bulged with a lump as big as a tennis ball: she had found the barb in it.

'Luckily he's not badly hurt,' said Kyria Eirini.

'He got a fright. I'm sorry,' Voula explained gratefully, because Kyria Eirini spoke no English. With a gasp of pain she squatted on her heels to face Barbara. 'It happen so quick!' she said tearfully; and met with shock a bitter relentless glare from Andoni.

'*Kakia* Voula!' Vassilaki hid his face.

'No, no, no,' said Barbara.

'But it was an accident,' said Kyria Eirini to everyone. 'These things happen. They can happen to anyone.'

The Kapetanissa gave her a grateful look. She had warned them about the *kapaki*, but this was not the time to say so; and besides she blamed all such accidents on the Evil Eye, but she could hardly say that either. Instead she hustled Voula home to take out the barb and dab vinegar on the sting, at the same time questioning her at length. Voula burst into more sobs: Andoni had blamed her without a word. She blamed herself, she told her mother, who stoutly told her she was being stupid. It was the Evil Eye, it was written, it was the will of God; she crossed herself.

'Yes, but they all hate me now,' said Voula.

Vassilaki, his sobs dwindling to sniffles and hiccups, was still clamped fast to Barbara on the floor. '*Ponaei*,' he whimpered now and then, when she tried to move; but it was clear that he wasn't badly hurt. When his grandmother knelt beside them with a bowl of milky antiseptic and a tuft of cotton wool, he knew what was coming: '*Ochi! Ochi! Ochi!*' he wailed, wriggling.

'Ach, *poulaki mou*.' His grandmother's eyes watered.

'I'll do it,' said Andoni.

'*Ochi!* Nao!'

'Vassilaki! Vassilaki *mou*!' His grandmother snapped on the light and ran up the steps, calling. He peered, blinking in the yellow glare, from behind his wet fists. '*Da da!*' she shouted, and punched the trapdoor. '*Da da to kapaki! Da! Da! Da!*'

Vassilaki gave a wheezy laugh. '*Da da pali*, Yiayia!' he commanded; so she beat it again, and again, until her arms ached and he decided that the *kapaki* was punished enough. And by then Andoni had swabbed the blood away.

As soon as Vassilaki was asleep Andoni inspected his head with a bright torch he had found, parting the damp tufts.

'He's all right. Really,' Barbara said.

'He could get delayed concussion,' muttered Andoni.

'I don't think so.'

'It's your job to look after him. Why did you leave it to Voula?'

'She offered. Vassilaki wanted her to take him.'

'He could have been killed.'

'It was an accident. It could have happened to anyone.'

'Did you call him to go up that way?'

'No, of course not!' Barbara jumped up.

'But you called him.'

'That was after he lifted it up.'

'I hope that's true.'

'I don't tell lies, Andoni.'

'You don't do anything much any more, do you?'

'No? Do you know why? I'm tired.'

'Tired!' He turned away.

'Tired, yes. Because I'm pregnant.'

It was some time before he turned to her; the torch in his hand threw winged shadows. He stood staring.

'You're not pleased.'

'Yes, I am. Yes. Are you sure? When will it be?'

'Mid–January, I think.'

'Does Mama know yet?'

'Most likely.'

He smiled at that.

'He's sleeping normally,' she said. 'He really will be all right.'

'I might just go for a walk, then. Just down to the *kafeneion* for a while, I'll burst if I stay here.' He bent over Vassilaki, then handed her the torch and went down into the street. From the balcony she watched him appear under each streetlamp, and disappear again.

After searching all over the sittingroom, she found her diary under a pile of *kilimia*, striped red and green and black, which she didn't remember having seen before; and took out the two pages of her letter to her sister. She had more to tell her. A moth flapped at the torch, its shadow rocking the gold walls.

> *P.S. Jilly, I'm pregnant. I was going to tell you when you were here, but somehow it never seemed to be the right time. They will wish me* kali eleftheria *when I tell them: it means* good freedom – *by which they mean good (easy) birth.*
>
> > *Be happy,*
> > *B.*

As they did every night, Voula and the Kapetanissa watched the boats get ready to go out in a jumble of nets and crates and lamps. Half the town was wandering along the waterfront and up and down the pier by then, dressed in their best for the *volta*. The streets were very dark now, except under the lights: people tripped over stones and tree roots. The sea held its oyster colours of yellow and grey longer, even when the caique and its little boats were chugging across to the fishing grounds, lamps strung in a row over the ringed wakes.

Later they sat with the families of the crew sharing bottles of beer and *ouzo* and plates of *mezedes* at the *kafeneion*. Moths fell against them. Often there was no other sound but the thump of the hurtling powdery moths. At every table children insisted, to the men's satisfaction, on sipping the froth from every glass of beer; soon they fell asleep in their mother's laps. Cats yowled under the chairs. Their fur twitching, they would put a calm paw on top of a cricket, then let it limp free, then cover it again. Their eyes flashed green. Beyond the yellow edges of the lamplight more crickets started creaking under the pines. Out at sea the boats gathered under a milky dome of colder light. A gull cried out; then another.

Voula, standing to pass her aunt a plate of *kalamari*, suddenly saw Andoni on the beach. But he looked away and walked on into the dark.

'Wasn't that your tenant? What's his name?' her aunt asked, munching loudly.

'No. I don't think so,' Voula said. She longed to be alone. Her stung thigh throbbed.

There were no lights on next door, when Voula and the Kapetanissa came home. They went straight to bed. The house was too hot for sleep, and held its heat and silence the whole night.

In the next room Vassilaki said in English a word like a bell, but woke only his grandmother. She could see the slatted moon from where she lay. There will be dew, she thought, by morning, and the houses will look like blocks of *feta* straight out of the brine, until the moon sets. At dawn they will be blue. I must wake Andoni to buy fish, she decided, because once the moon is full the boats know better than to go out with their little lamps. For a week we'll be without fish.

It was too hot to sleep, and besides she was no longer sleepy, having gone to bed earlier than usual when Barbara did. They had sat in the light of an amber lamp in the kitchen and eaten cold what was left of the *imam bayildi*, just the two of them mopping their plates with bread and talking quietly, almost secretively. They felt fonder of each other than they had for a long time, and they both knew this, and so were shy with each other. She thought of asking Barbara if she might be pregnant, but it was not the right time yet. When Vassilaki woke tousled and grizzling, they soothed and dandled him. They spoonfed him an egg that she soft-boiled in the coffee *briki* and on which Barbara drew a naughty face, a little Vassilaki. His pallor was gone. He sipped the egg greedily and then ate some bread with grainy honey and a peach like a yellow rose that she had saved for him. She wanted to read Barbara a prayer from the *Theia Litourgeia*, but the lamplight, heavy with moths and beetles, was making her eyes sore. They are like fish in a yellow sea, Barbara said, waving insects away. They carried Vassilaki, fast asleep, up the outside stairs to bed. She heard Andoni come up soon after.

For all she knew, good might have come of the child's fall, since Andoni blamed the girl for it; though who knew how long the good would last or what harm might come of it? In any case, it was not how she would have gone about it. The child hurt, the girl stung, the bee dead. A bee had come blundering into the sun out of the Panagia *sta Melissia*. Was it that bee? Was a bee's life of so little account to the Panagia, that she sent it to die? Thy will be done: she crossed herself. It's not for me to say. Maybe our lives are of no more account than a bee's, if the truth be known.

She must nail up the *kapaki* in the morning.

Out in the night a click of hoofs and a faint 'meh' made her sigh. There was a goat loose again. It must have come for the rest of the Kapetanissa's climbing beans; it would finish the lot off tonight, no doubt, and the Kapetanissa would talk of nothing else tomorrow. How did the Garden of Eden ever survive with goats in it? Goats eat every green shoot that pokes up. They're a ruin, goats are, though the milk makes up for it.

Is that bee alive now in the next world, she wondered; and is there honey there? Water, and milk and eggs, bread and wine? Shall we all have other forms, or none and be made of air? We boil wheat with sugar to make the *kollyva* for the dead; but it's only we, the living, who eat it. Or so it seems. For us of this world, at least, it tastes good, salty and sweet together. Like sardines fried in sweet green oil; or watermelon with a slab of briny *feta*, or any dry cheese; honey on rough bread; grapes, rich heavy muscat grapes, dipped in the sea to wash them.

Pain is like salt, in a way, she thought; it can make the sweetness stronger, unless there's too much of it. Pain and sorrow and loss.

There was too much salt in the *imam bayildi* today. Never mind. Well.

My poor Vassili, whose sins are forgiven: that was a salty old joke he loved to tell, the one about honey. Only a man could have made that joke up. A man might even believe it, who knows?

A gypsy (he put on a wheedling voice) came to an old widow, I forget why, and said, 'What is your wish, my lady? I can give you one of two things. A fine young man to marry, or a pot of honey. Just tell me which you want.'

'Now what sort of a choice do you call that?' (And he cackled like an old widow.) 'I couldn't eat the honey, could I? There's not a tooth in my head, is there?' (At which he laughed angrily as if he knew all about old widows, and disliked what he knew.)

She breathed deeply of the shuttered air, cooler now with the dew towards daybreak, and pulled the rough sheet up over her folded throat. In the next world may we all be young again, she fell asleep wishing. All of us young and at peace by the sea for ever.

MILK

Beverley Farmer

Whether writing about being an Australian woman in love in Greece, or waiting at the airport for a small son, or being old and embedded in everything that has gone before, Beverley Farmer isolates moments of human experience with almost unbearable clarity.

These are deceptively simple, extraordinarily attractive stories, set in Greece and Australia by a gifted and original writer.

Winner of the 1984 NSW Premier's Award for Fiction

ALONE

Beverley Farmer

Alone is the haunting and utterly sensual record of a young woman's passion for her lover, Catherine – and of her terrifying isolation as her anguish becomes absolute. First published in 1980, this novel brought Beverley Farmer immediate acclaim.

THE CHILDREN'S BACH

Helen Garner

Athena and Dexter lead a frumpish, happy family life, sheltered from the tackier aspects of the modern world and bound by duty towards a disturbed child.

Their comfortable rut is disrupted by the arrival of Elizabeth, a tough nut from Dexter's past. She brings with her Vicki, her lonely teenage sister, who looks for a mother in Athena; Philip, her charming, talented, evasive man; and Poppy, Philip's twelve-year-old daughter, one of those prematurely wise children that a broken marriage can produce, a puritan who casts a cool eye on the disreputable antics of her elders.

In the upheaval Athena sees a way out: it leads into a world whose casual egotism she has dreamed of without being able to imagine its consequences.

'Helen Garner gets better and better . . .'
Weekend Australian

'Helen Garner's latest book, *The Children's Bach*, is a beautiful piece of fiction.'
Meanjin

SCISSION

Tim Winton

Tim Winton writes of people struggling with change and dis-integration, he writes of excruciating moments when love and loss are sharply focussed, and of a world that is somehow made more real for being slightly out of whack.

'Tim Winton is a classicist, a master of passion restrained by form, dealing with the agonies and ecstasies of family life.'
Sydney Morning Herald